The Decision Paperback Copyright © 2021 Lorhainne Ekelund
Editor: Talia Leduc

All rights reserved.
ISBN-13: 978-1990590160

Give feedback on the book at:
lorhainneeckhart@hotmail.com

Twitter: @LEckhart
Facebook: AuthorLorhainneEckhart

Printed in the U.S.A

THE DECISION

The Friessens (Brad & Emily)

LORHAINNE ECKHART

Runaway (Andy and Laura)
Overdue
The Unexpected Storm (Neil and Candy)
The Wedding (Neil and Candy)

The Friessens: A New Beginning

The Deadline (Andy and Laura)
The Price to Love (Neil and Candy)
A Different Kind of Love (Brad and Emily)
A Vow of Love, A Friessen Family Christmas

The Friessens

The Reunion
The Bloodline (Andy & Laura)
The Promise (Diana & Jed)
The Business Plan (Neil & Candy)
The Decision (Brad & Emily)
First Love (Katy)
Family First
Leave the Light On
In the Moment
In the Family: A Friessen Family Christmas
In the Silence
In the Stars
In the Charm
Unexpected Consequences
It Was Always You
The First Time I Saw You
Welcome to My Arms
Welcome to Boston
I'll Always Love You
Ground Rules

A Reason to Breathe
You Are My Everything
Anything For You
The Homecoming includes FREE short story When They
Were Young
Stay Away From My Daughter
The Bad Boy
A Place to Call Our Own
The Visitor
All About Devon
Long Past Dawn
How to Heal a Heart
Keep Me In Your Heart

"Real romance that touches the heart…feels so real that you can't help but get emotional…a fantastic read."

A. Brantley

One of the best series I have ever read about family that sticks together no matter what differences they may have."

Cathy

"A fantastic story that hit home."

Judy

The Friessens Family

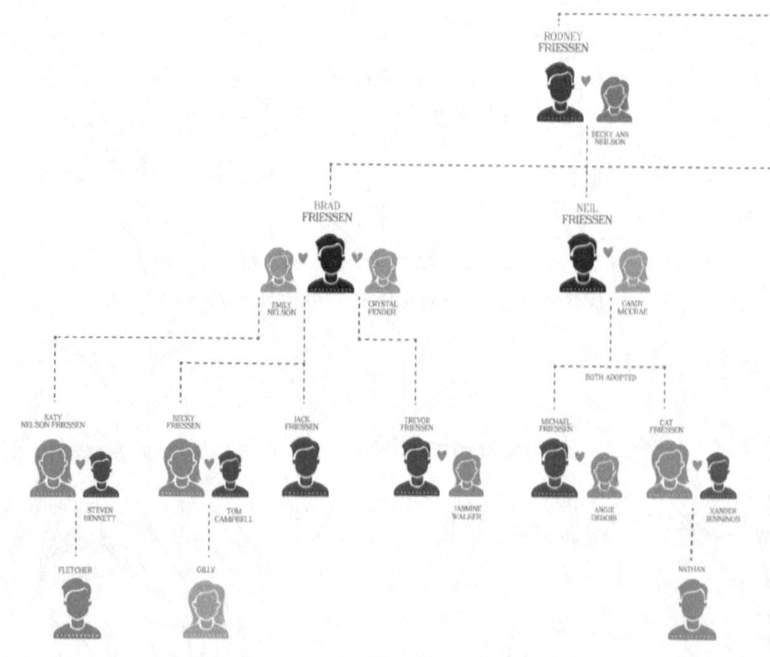

The Outsider	
THE FORGOTTEN CHILD	BRAD & EMILY
A BABY AND A WEDDING	BRAD & EMILY & *the most tad Neil Rodney & Becky*
FALLEN HERO	JED, DIANA & ANDY
THE SEARCH	JED, DIANA & ANDY
THE AWAKENING	ANDY & LAURA

The Outsider	
SECRETS	DIANA & JED *with the entire Friessen Family*
RUNAWAY	ANDY & LAURA
OVERDUE	JED & DIANA
THE UNEXPECTED STORM	NEIL & CANDY
THE WEDDING	NEIL & CANDY *and the entire Friessen Family*

The Friessens: A New Beginning

THE DEADLINE	ANDY & LAURA
THE PRICE TO LOVE	NEIL & CANDY
A DIFFERENT KIND OF LOVE	BRAD & EMILY
A VOW OF LOVE	THE ENTIRE
A FRIESSEN FAMILY CHRISTMAS	FRIESSEN FAMILY

TODD
FRIESSEN
CAROLINE
McCAIN

JED
FRIESSEN
DIANA
CLAREMONT
FULTON

ANDY
FRIESSEN
LAURA
PARNELL

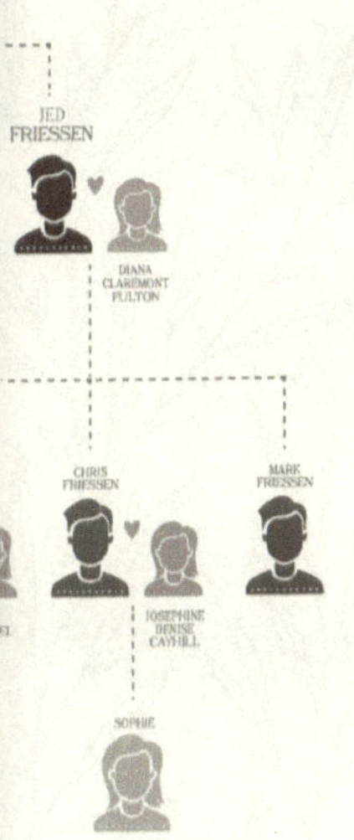

CHRIS
FRIESSEN
JOSEPHINE
DENISE
CAYHILL

MARK
FRIESSEN

JEREMY
FRIESSEN
TIFFY
CAHILL

CHELSEA
FRIESSEN
ALARIC
TAFT

SARA
FRIESSEN

ZAC
FRIESSEN

GABRIEL
FRIESSEN
ELIZABETH
ABERCROMBIE

SOPHIE

BRANDON

SHAUNTY

Friessens

THE ENTIRE FRIESSEN FAMILY	
ANDY & LAURA	
JED & DIANA	
NEIL & CANDY	
BRAD & EMILY	
KATY & STEVEN	
KATY & STEVEN	

The Friessens

LEAVE THE LIGHT ON	KATY & STEVEN
IN THE MOMENT	BECKY & TOM *introducing you to a new character Vic McCabe which then launches a new series, The McCabe Brothers*
IN THE FAMILY *A Friessen Family Christmas*	THE ENTIRE FRIESSEN FAMILY
IN THE SILENCE	CAT & XANDER
IN THE STARS	DANNY & EVIE
IN THE CHARM	CHRIS & J.D.
UNEXPECTED CONSEQUENCES	CHRIS & J.D. *and Danny & Evie*

The Friessens

IT WAS ALWAYS YOU	KATY & STEVEN
THE FIRST TIME I SAW YOU	GABRIEL & ELIZABETH
WELCOME TO MY ARMS	CHELSEA & ALARIC
WELCOME TO BOSTON	PAIGE & MORGAN *(a Friessen Justice short story)*
I'LL ALWAYS LOVE YOU	JEREMY
GROUND RULES	JEREMY & TIFFY
A REASON TO BREATHE	TREVOR
YOU ARE MY EVERYTHING	MICHAEL

The Friessens, stars of the bestselling series, are back with ***THE DECISION***, another heartwarming fan favorite romance from ***New York Times*** and ***USA Today*** **bestselling author Lorhainne Eckhart.**

Emily Friessen has everything a woman could want: a husband who's the love of her life, a family that stands together, and children she wouldn't trade for anything. To everyone around her, she's confident and strong—but then, she has to be with a man like Brad, who is all about family and too handsome for his own good.

Emily isn't as together as she appears, though, and when life throws her and Brad a curveball, it tests their relationship, leaving Emily scrambling and feeling very much alone as both are faced with a decision no parent should have to make.

Chapter 1

Brad walked the ridge overlooking his land, taking in the browns and golds of the drying pasture to the tree line, where the forest thickened and thinned closer to the many outbuildings, big and small, on his ranch—a ranch that had been in his family for generations. This was Friessen land, and being the eldest son to Rodney Friessen, he had inherited everything. At the time, Brad had never questioned how only he, the eldest of three, could have all this. That was what happened in families: The eldest son inherited the earth. Was that not the saying?

His brother Jed, the youngest, had been left to set out on his own and had bought a piece of shit property in Snohomish County, where he had built something from nothing. Jed was pigheaded, at times so closed off that Brad wondered what he was thinking, but he loved him. He loved all his family. His father had retired down in Cancun, having bought a huge ranching operation on the Yucatan Peninsula with his brother Neil, a Harvard graduate who owned a multimillion-dollar resort. Brad, meanwhile, had been handed all of this, and at times he wondered whether he had earned any of it. Yes, he worked hard, but he'd never had to work to gain something, to create something.

He'd never considered himself fortunate or privileged. He'd never thought much of it until recently. Maybe it was age, becoming older and wiser. He smiled to himself, wondering, if it were possible, would he go back and change anything, trade in all the pain, the heartache…and the love he had now? No, he supposed he wouldn't. All the choices he'd made, both good and bad, had brought him here. They had brought him Emily, their children, and a life filled with struggles. It had been a bumpy road, but he wouldn't trade his family for anything. He had everything he could ever want.

Being a rancher, one could say, was in his blood. He didn't want to do anything else. He was a part owner of his brother's fancy resort in Cancun, but, as he'd said to Neil, as long as he didn't have to take part in the daily operations, that was fine with him. There was one thing Brad understood and knew deep down that many people didn't, something people struggled and searched for their entire lives. This was where he belonged, on this fertile rock in the Pacific Northwest, with his land. The only problem was that Angus Friessen, his grandfather, being old, Irish, and proud of it, had added an addendum on the property that it could only pass to the eldest son—not the daughter! What the man had been thinking was beyond Brad. Considering times had changed, it seemed over the top even to him.

He realized, as he took in the vast acreage, with a spectacular view of the pastures below, the grazing cattle, the field of hay, and his horses, that having a male heir was going to be a problem, as his son, his only son, had autism.

He took a deep breath, seeing his ranch hands and a dusty trail in the distance. He had to squint to see who was coming, but then, it was late afternoon. The kids would be home soon. It had to be the school bus pulling in. Trevor, Katy, and Becky, his youngest, would be racing down the driveway and turning their once quiet house into a lively affair for Emily. With only a few weeks left until the end of the school year, they needed to have a heart to heart about what was next for Trevor. Emily had already mentioned it four times. (Brad had heard her the first time, but she'd needed to repeat herself because he hadn't replied.)

Trevor would be seventeen soon, and the girls were growing up fast, too. From Emily's first marriage, Katy was a year younger than Trevor and was blond and slender, with a young lady's figure that was turning the heads of a few young boys, who were calling all the time. It was giving Brad a few gray hairs as he considered, now, how to handle his girls. It was time he and Emily sat Katy down and laid out the rules for dating. Of course, he wouldn't hesitate to put the fear of God into each and every one of those boys who came knocking. Becky, their little girl, was just entering her teenage years. He'd already noticed the change in attitude, as she was giving Emily more lip than before, testing her boundaries. He needed to have a chat with her, too.

Maybe that was why he'd spent the last week walking the ridgeline, looking over the property as he did his best to get his head on straight and figure out what was next. He felt for the first time that they were fast wading into the new and different territory of raising two teenage girls and a young autistic man. What to do? Tonight he'd take Emily aside and they'd make some decisions about what was next for their family.

And this land.

He took in the trail he'd climbed up and slung his rifle over his shoulder just as his cell phone rang. He reached for it from his back pocket and saw "Home" displayed there, smiling because Emily was probably wondering where he'd gone off to. "On my way," he started.

"Dad!" Katy cried out in a tone that had the hair standing up on the back of his neck.

"Whoa, what's going on?"

"It's Trevor, Dad. Mom said to call you and get you back here. Someone hurt him…" She was starting to ramble on and heading toward hysterics, and he couldn't understand a word she was saying.

"Katy, stop it, calm down. I'm heading back to the house." He was running down the trail, sliding sideways in spots with the phone to his ear. "How bad is he hurt? Put your mom on!" He knew he was shouting, but he couldn't do a damn thing, being this far from the house, and that made him furious.

"I can't put Mom on. She has Trevor upstairs. She's trying to stop the bleeding. It's horrible, Dad." He could hear the edge in her voice, and of course his head was going to some pretty bad places.

This was one of those times, as he broke the tree line, that he wanted to kick himself in the ass for not saddling a horse. "Did she call an ambulance?"

There was silence for a minute.

"Katy!" Brad yelled into the phone as he waved in the air to Cliff, who was on the tractor, but then thought better of it. He started running toward the house, pounding the ground, his rifle over his shoulder.

"No," Katy said, sounding confused.

In that second, as he got closer to the house, he realized something wasn't quite right.

"Why not?" he said into the phone as he raced up the

back steps, hanging up the phone and seeing Katy in the kitchen, standing and holding the phone to her ear. "Em!" He shouted as he took in Katy, pale, wide eyed, looking to him and then the phone and then hanging it up. He was out of breath, sweating as he rested his hand on her shoulder. Just then, there was a squeak on the stairs.

"Daddy!" Becky raced down. "You should see all the blood from Trevor." She seemed excited and impressed, and Brad wanted answers.

"Brad, up here! Emily said. "Trevor has a nose bleed."

Seriously? He glared down at Katy, who was standing there and shrugging. "A nose bleed," he said. "We're going to have a talk later about your dramatics."

He walked to the back door, opened the gun cabinet, and unloaded the rifle before setting it back in, locking the cabinet up, and putting the key in his pocket. He started up the stairs and into the bathroom, where Trevor was holding a wet cloth to his nose. There was blood on his yellow T-shirt, but he appeared far from hurt.

"Hi, Dad," he said in a nasal tone, smiling as he pulled the cloth away. His nose was still dripping and appeared a little pink but not swollen. Otherwise he looked fine.

"What's going on here? I get this panicked call from Katy that Trevor is hurt, was beat up or something bad, and she made it sound as if he needed to go to Emergency."

Emily had spots of fresh blood on her sleeveless pale blue shirt, her brown hair pinned up in a messy bun. She raised an eyebrow, shaking her head. "No, I didn't get the whole story from Katy, though, as she pulled Trevor in, both her and Becky. All they said was that he'd been hurt on the bus. I told her to call you and get you back here so we could find out who we need to hunt down." She sounded really mad, and he could see she was probably jumping to conclusions, considering they weren't getting the entire story.

"Girls, get up here!" Brad called out. "Trevor, what happened?"

"I fell," he said, then looked in the mirror as if studying his nose.

"What is it?" Katy appeared with her sister behind her. They were both staring at Trevor.

"Katy, I didn't tell you to call your dad and scare him, making him think the worst had happened with Trevor. I don't understand why you'd do that."

She shrugged. "Sorry, but it was a lot of blood, Mom. Even you were worried when you saw it."

"It was really gross," Becky added.

"We're going to talk later about that, Katy, but right now I want to know what happened here. Trevor, you said you fell?" Brad rested his hand on Trevor's shoulder as Emily leaned in, fussing again, dabbing at his nose with another cloth.

"Katy tripped me."

"I did not trip you, Trevor!" she yelled out, sounding truly affronted.

"Oops, sorry, my mistake," he said and laughed.

"It was Deanna Miller. She's in grade twelve. I saw her stick her foot out when Trevor went past, and she tripped him. She's not very nice," Becky said. "I heard her talking with that awful Jason Cresswell, saying they needed to take down the idiot."

Brad was trying to figure out who these kids were, and he found himself looking to Emily and then over to Katy. He was stuck on the "idiot" part. What kid would say something so hurtful, so wrong?

"It's okay," Trevor said, putting the washcloth in the hamper.

"No, it's not okay, Trevor," Brad said. "If someone hurt you, you have to say something. Tell us, did this Deanna trip you?"

Trevor just shrugged. "I don't know."

"Dad, I was ahead of Trevor when he fell," Katy said. "I didn't see it, but Deanna is not nice. Trevor, you shouted when you fell. I helped you up, and you were holding your nose, and there was blood pouring out. I heard the bus driver asking all the kids what happened when we got off."

"She was really mad," Becky added.

"Who is Jason Cresswell? I don't think I know him," Emily said. Trevor was now looking in the mirror, examining the side of his nose.

"He's in grade eleven. He's a bully. I don't like him," Becky said.

"I think maybe I need to go and have a talk with the school," Emily said.

"How about, since we're not rushing off to the emergency room now and everyone appears to be okay, you go work on your homework?" Brad said to the kids. "I'm going to have a talk with your mom."

"I don't have homework, Dad," Becky said.

"I don't have homework, either," Trevor announced.

Katy was frowning. "That's so not fair. Why do I have to have it all piled on me? Trevor never gets anything." She was crossing her arms as if she wanted to argue her point.

"That's because he has autism," Becky added with dramatics, rolling her eyes.

"Okay, enough. Katy, go do your homework," Emily said. "I know you haven't finished that book report you were supposed to do. Oh, yes, I got an email today from your teacher. Becky, go read a book. Trevor, you too." She took a breath, sounding as if she was nearing the end of her rope.

Brad took in the large main bathroom with its dated tub and shower. "So, sounds like we have a problem with some kids picking on Trevor," he said. Emily turned and stared at him, firming her lips, appearing frustrated as she walked out of the bathroom and into their large master suite. Brad followed, closing the door behind him as Emily pulled off the bloody shirt and tossed it in with the dirty clothes. She lifted a peach T-shirt out of their six-drawer chest and pulled it on.

"You're not answering me now," he said. He couldn't believe she'd walked away from him, and he was trying to figure out what was going through her head when she turned around and stumbled a bit.

"Em!" He reached her before she fell, lifting her in his arms, resting her on the bed. She was pale and had an odd look on her face as she widened her eyes and blinked.

When she looked up at him, she said, "I'm pregnant."

Chapter 2

____

The expression on Brad's face was one of shock, as if he hadn't heard right. Of course he had, but she hadn't meant to tell him like this. Not right now, anyway.

"Wow," he said, staring down at her, his hands on his hips. She lay back and rested her arm over her forehead.

"Yeah, wow is right."

"When did you find out?" he asked. She didn't miss how he seemed to be taking in all of her as if deciding how best to bubble wrap her and tuck her in, as if she needed safekeeping—which she didn't, not by a longshot.

"I haven't yet, officially. I'm late."

He stiffened and gestured with his hand. "Wait a second. You think you're pregnant, or you know you're pregnant, which is it?" The way he watched her, she knew he was trying to figure out what was going on in her head, what she was thinking. Sometimes she wondered whether his first thought was always that she was overreacting. The fact was she'd been worrying about a lot of things lately.

"I just figured it out this morning when I was cleaning

out the fridge. There was this awful odor." She waved her hand and swallowed. Just thinking of it made the bile rise. She could still smell the odor of rotting fish. Even though she'd emptied the entire fridge expecting to find the culprit shoved way in the back, it hadn't been. It had, in fact, been reasonably clean. She'd then turned her nose up at a second cup of coffee and wondered for a second, counting, realizing how late she was.

Brad appeared confused.

"Odors always set me off, or they did," she said.

"It sounds like a trip to the doctor is in order," Brad replied, sitting on the bed as she slipped off, going to look at her face in the dresser mirror. She had dark circles under her eyes, too. Being tired was another sign. "I'm getting too old to have kids. A baby at our age… Brad, the kids are all in school now, and I have my time back." She turned to face him, feeling truly awful for saying that. "Does that make me horrible? I love our kids, but I don't miss the busyness that goes along with it, the late-night feedings, being sleep deprived, diapers." She was feeling depressed all of a sudden, and when she glanced up, Brad was on his feet, walking across the carpet toward her. "I just vacuumed, Brad," she said as she took in his scuffed western boots. He didn't seem to care, as he just shook his head.

"Forget the floor. You just dropped a bomb that you're pregnant but don't know for sure, and here you are, on top of this, worried because…" He stopped talking. Of course she could tell he was irritated with her. "I'm not getting it, Em. Is it that you don't want any more kids? Is that what you're saying?" He moved closer to her, stopping just in front of her. This time, by the way he held himself back, she could see how her bringing up all her unresolved issues had tossed him a curveball. He was taking it all wrong.

Emily shook her head, placing her hands on her face,

wondering whether her expression showed the misery she was feeling. "No, that's not what I'm saying. I just didn't expect this, Brad. Do you have any idea how embarrassing it would be to show up at the kids' high school and walk in pregnant?"

He looked away as if he still didn't get it. For a moment, she sensed the distance between them. "Who cares? Seriously, Em."

"I care, and the other mothers care. I remember, just last week, I listened to two of them go on about one of the moms walking out with her teenage son, and she was about ready to give birth. They ridiculed her, made jokes about her, laughed—not to her face, but they were nasty, and I just..." She wanted to cry, thinking of being the odd woman out.

The way he was staring at her had her swallowing. It was as if he didn't know who she was. "I've never seen you this shallow, Em. Why would you ever let a bunch of small-minded women bother you? This is our baby, for the love of God. I cannot believe you." He was furious with her. He didn't get it. She was trying to share her feelings, but maybe she shouldn't have.

What she did do was instinctive, wrapping her arms across her stomach. "It hurts to be talked about like that, and knowing it would be me makes me ache. I'm not that thick skinned, Brad. Women can be vicious is all I'm saying."

He was shaking his head still. How could she get him to understand her perspective even if he didn't agree? She glanced down at her fingers as her throat thickened. Why was she letting this bother her so much?

Then he was there in front of her, but she wouldn't look up at him. He slipped his finger under her chin and tilted it up. Maybe he was trying to understand as he held his hand there, sliding his fingers around her chin, holding her in a way that was comforting and forced her to look at him. "And because of these women, are you telling me you wouldn't have another baby?"

He really didn't get it. She pushed his hand down. "Don't be ridiculous. Of course I would. Besides, I should really take a pregnancy test, get it confirmed, and then…"

"Whoa, stop," Brad interrupted her, holding up his hand. He laughed at her. "Em, there's one thing I know about you. You never act this flighty." He laughed again.

For the first time ever, she felt as if Brad was insulting her. She was about to snap some smart remark back, and maybe he sensed that, pulling her toward him, wrapping his arms around her as his hand slid over her bottom. He brought his face closer. He was holding her so she couldn't get away, pressed close to him. She could feel every hard part of him. She couldn't fight him like this. He was being unfair, and maybe he knew it, as he grinned like a fool, trying to kiss her. He was teasing her.

"Brad, I'm mad at you. I'm not flighty. How could you call me that? It's insulting."

He pressed a kiss to her and again grinned, running his hands over her ass so she could feel him.

"Not fair." She looped her arms around his shoulders and was leaning up to kiss him when the door opened.

"Mom!" Trevor called out. "Don't do that."

Brad loosened his hold as Emily jumped, turning around.

Trevor walked out the door, calling out over his shoulder, "What's for dinner?" He didn't wait for her to answer.

"We need to put a lock on that door," Brad said as he leaned in again, this time wrapping his arms around her front, his hands flattening over her stomach and pulling her close. He kissed her neck, his breath warm in her ear.

"Tonight, you can make this disruption up to me." Then he started to walk away after patting her ass again. He called out to Trevor and Becky as he jogged down the stairs.

Emily glanced into the mirror again, taking in the tiny lines around her eyes and mouth, which seemed deeper than they had been the day before.

Chapter 3

"I don't know why you insist we go to the doctor," Emily said. "I can just pick up one of those home pregnancy tests and be done with it. Then we wouldn't be wasting time. We both have so much to do, and I still need to stop in to the school and have a talk with the teachers about those two hooligans."

Brad glanced to Emily and back to the road. She was off again today. He'd noticed it the night before when he'd come to bed and she'd been out cold. He couldn't in good conscience have woken her, as he couldn't remember ever seeing her so tired.

"You haven't been to the doctor in a long time."

"Not true. I was there just last week for the girls' check-up," she snapped right back.

"Yes, for the girls, not for you." He needed to get her to see that she was always looking after everyone else, putting everybody else first. "You look after all of us, Em, and never once have I seen you put yourself first. I love you for your unselfishness, but, honey, to give everything you have to us, you have to look after yourself first. With every disaster, you know that's the first thing they tell you: You first. To be clear, you're going to the doctor, and he's going to check you out thoroughly so you're one hundred percent okay. Have a pregnancy test done by a real doctor so he can confirm you are, in fact, pregnant!" He hadn't realized he was shouting a bit. Emily just stared him down, and he noticed the tinge of gray under her eyes.

"Brad, I'm okay, and I have things to do. I really need to go in to the school. Maybe there're some problems no one has told us about. I mean, you know we're being restricted more and more lately, and they tell us very little. If they're tripping Trevor on a school bus, what's to say it's not happening at school and they're just not telling us?"

He reached across the seat for her hand, giving it a squeeze to settle her down before pulling it away. "I need you to back up. Remember what I said a second ago about looking after you first? This is what I'm talking about. You're going to the doctor first. School is second, and I'm thinking, depending on what the doctor says, I'll handle that myself." He was thinking of maybe taking her home and sticking her in bed for some sleep.

"Brad, you're the last person who should be going in to the school. The way some of the staff push your buttons has set you off more than a few times. Remember, being calm and not reacting is important, and you scare them," she added.

"Well, maybe sometimes a few of them need to be scared, thinking they can do whatever they want, as if they know better." There had been a few teachers in the mix and a support worker who had refused to work with Trevor's consultant, within the parameters of his program-ming, and had refused to understand that Trevor could and would meet each challenge. It had been frustrating, and he had, in hindsight, lost his temper. His wife hadn't, though. She'd sucked it up and said nothing even though he'd seen how much it hurt her. Instead, she'd taken it out on the laundry at home.

She was looking out the window as Brad pulled into the lot by the clinic where their family doctor, Randall Keys, practiced. Emily still hadn't said anything, and she appeared distracted as she undid her seatbelt and went to open the door. He reached over and took her arm. "Hey."

When she looked over to him, she seemed to be holding on to a lot.

"When have we ever kept things from each other?" he said. He didn't miss her frown, and he slid his fingers over her cheek so she couldn't turn away.

"I know, I'm sorry. I just feel so unsettled, and I don't know why. I'm nervous." She bit her lip again, and he wouldn't let her look away. He watched tears pop up in her eyes before she blinked furiously to clear them.

"Why? Is this about being pregnant and the school thing again?" He couldn't understand what was going through her head. She was jumping between worried, scared, rushed, and he didn't know what. Emily just shook her head after pulling her lower lip between her teeth. She appeared conflicted. That was the only thing he could think of.

"No." She shook her head and leaned into his hand. "Forget I said anything. I'm just overthinking." This time she managed a smile, one that didn't meet her eyes, and the lightness in her tone seemed forced. He knew there was something else, and he didn't want to let it go, but she didn't give him a chance as she pulled away and slipped out, closing the door behind her.

Chapter 4

Emily was wearing her leather slip-on Clarks with a one-inch heel, the nice ones that went with her new low-rise wranglers and a salmon colored tank top. She also had on a thick leather belt with a jeweled buckle, one of the many gifts Brad had bought her for Christmas the previous year. She caught a glimpse of herself in the lobby floor-to-ceiling mirror as she walked in, and she looked great, with her trim figure, her hair hanging loose in waves halfway down her back. For the first time, she realized she wasn't dressing and looking like a mom. She liked this look, including the sight of her hunky husband behind her. He was dressed as he always was, in jeans, a plaid blue shirt with a jean jacket overtop, and scuffed cowhide boots. His short dark hair was threaded with more and more gray, but it was damn appealing, a look he could pull off. Not a woman around could walk past him without giving a second look. That was just the effect he had on women, including her, as she stood so close to him she could feel his heat. The fact was they looked great together.

Brad jabbed the elevator button and slipped his hand into his pocket, the other on the small of her back, staring at her in the glass. She knew why. She'd slipped out of the truck, evading his question only because she didn't understand why she was so conflicted. She loved her husband, her children, their life. Brad was the love of her life, and being with him, being loved by him was beyond anything she could have ever imagined. At times she still wondered how she'd gotten so lucky as to find someone like him. Even though there were days the man tested her patience, her sound reasoning, she wouldn't have traded a moment of it for anything.

The seconds ticked on, and he was still watching her with those amazing eyes filled with such heat, love, and deep emotion. They hid that part of himself that he shared with no one but her, and she knew that holding things back from him was pointless, as he seemed to be waiting her out. He could wait all day, to a point, and she knew it was only a matter of time before he started working her down to find out what was going through her head. That would be when the fight started, though their fights always ended with her whimpering under him. Thankfully, the elevator dinged and she stepped in, him right behind her, and jabbed the button to the second floor. His arm slid around her.

"We need to discuss this, Em. I don't like seeing you like this."

Damn him, he could be so persuasive. She leaned back, needing him more than before. The door opened, and she had to let out a breath as Brad slid his hand over her ass, squeezing it as if he knew exactly what she was thinking. Then he patted her butt. "Come on, let's go."

She moved out of the elevator. He was right behind her. "Brad, could you stop? I don't want to discuss this anymore, not right now. I just want to get this doctor's visit over with." She hoped Brad would be sidetracked and let it drop, all her unresolved issues. She wanted time and space to run them through her mind. Some things, a girl should keep to herself.

Brad reached around her and opened the door to the doctor's office, which opened into a large square waiting room with blue walls and dark blue carpeting. Black cloth chairs lined one wall, and there were half a dozen women with kids waiting. Brad walked with her to the counter at the side to check in, his hand resting beside her.

"Hi, I'm Emily Friessen," Emily said to the receptionist, a plain woman with brown hair in a ponytail and a white top. "I have an appointment with Dr. Keys."

"Oh, yes, I have your file right here." The woman smiled, glancing to Brad, a sparkle in her eyes. Her smile deepened.

Emily wanted to snarl. She couldn't shake her territorial feeling as the hair prickled on the back of her neck. "This is my husband," she said, though she didn't know why she needed to point it out. She reached over and touched his hand. Maybe he knew, as he squeezed her fingers, standing so close his legs brushed hers.

The nurse appeared not to notice her response. She said, "I have a room ready for you and can take you right in. I'll get you to leave a urine sample, and we'll run a pregnancy test while you wait." She stood up with a file and started around the corner, and Brad made no move to sit down.

"You're coming?" she asked, looking up at him, at the same time not wanting him to sit out here for all these women to ogle.

He gave her one of his looks as if she was crazy for asking. He wasn't a man who sat and waited. "Oh, yeah."

She was taken into a tiny exam room and given a cloth gown. The nurse opened the door to the attached bathroom. "The doctor will be right in. Just leave the sample in the cup on the shelf."

Emily put the gown on the exam table as the door closed and then stepped into the bathroom. She left the sample and put it on the shelf in the cupboard so they could access it from the other side, then pulled open the door and undressed before slipping on the gown, leaving her socks on as she hopped up on the exam table. Brad just leaned against the counter, and she realized how small this room was with her husband here. "I don't remember you ever tagging along like this to the doctor's before," she said.

"There's a first time for everything," he replied as he looked around. "So, while we wait, why don't you tell me what's going on in that head of yours? I can't remember you ever walking away like you did. You holding on to something, Em." He gestured between them. "You know that's not what we do."

His arms were crossed now as he leaned against the counter, watching her, expecting her to come clean and explain her confused thoughts and emotions. He was so damn attractive, and he was far from a pushover. It had always been his eyes, that whiskey-colored heat that simmered, filled with love, passion, so much feeling for her. She had to shut her eyes, because that part of him always had her wavering when she was trying to stand her ground. She glanced away for a second but looked back at him a moment later because she knew he'd be in her face otherwise, not letting her turn away.

"That's the problem, Brad. I'm not keeping anything from you. I just can't explain or make sense of this feeling I have. It's unsettled. Maybe it's because I'm tired, and realizing I'm pregnant…"

He leaned forward. "Let the doctor confirm you're pregnant before you start—"

The door opened before Brad could finish, and her heart started hammering as if she were being faced with her executioner, with the prospect of having all her suspicions answered. What was wrong with her? This shouldn't be a bad thing.

"Emily, I see it's now your turn. Just saw you with the kids." The doctor reached out and shook Brad's hand. "Brad, haven't seen you in some time. How've you been?"

"Pretty good, actually. How about you, Doc? Looks like your practice is really picking up."

Dr. Keys was tall, with a shaved head, blue eyes, and a stunning smile that had, at times, made her uneasy, maybe because he was so handsome. She was so in love with her husband that she felt awkward noticing that.

He looked from Brad to Emily and down at Emily's file. "You suspect you're pregnant?" He pulled over a round stool on wheels and sat down, pulling out a pen from his red dress shirt. His dark pants rose up and showed off red, white, and blue checked socks. Odd, but it seemed to work.

"She does," Brad said. Emily just sat there, her hands resting in her lap, her legs dangling over the edge of the exam table. She realized then that both men were watching her as if it was her turn to speak.

"Have you taken a home pregnancy test?" Dr. Keys asked.

"No," she said, then cleared her throat.

"When was your last cycle?"

She glanced up at Brad, who was watching her intently. The problem was that it had been so long, she wasn't sure now. She opened her mouth to answer, but nothing came out.

"Okay, let me just check on those results." He pulled open the door and stepped out.

Emily found herself searching Brad out, not missing the humor in his expression. "It's not funny."

"It actually is," he said just as the doctor came back in and shut the door.

"Looks like congratulations are in order, Mom and Dad. You're having a baby. Let's get you checked out and find out how far along you are."

Brad was all smiles. He was happy, of course, but she, for the first time in her life, was feeling shell shocked at this news. She didn't know how to feel or what to feel as she sat on the edge of the table and scooted around, wondering why she couldn't feel the same joy as Brad. She did the only thing she could think of: pasted a smile on her face, lay down, and tried to push every question, doubt, and uncertainty away.

"Okay, here we go," she whispered.

Chapter 5

Emily not only refused to stay in bed when they arrived home, she insisted on heading into the kitchen and baking. He was about to argue with her and insist she lie down and nap because of the dark circles, and because the doctor had advised her to take some me time and rest, but the problem was that once she got an idea in her head, she could be mighty stubborn.

He had to chalk it up to the fact that they'd learned Emily was further along than expected, fifteen weeks. How he'd not noticed was beyond him, considering their sex life was extraordinary. He knew her body and her cycle almost as well as she did. Maybe it was everything they had on their plate—the kids, the ranch, and now partnering with Neil in that fancy resort of his down in Cancun. Maybe they both needed some time to step back from all the busyness of life.

Brad was pleased the doctor had given Emily a thorough exam and then sat them down to talk about a number of genetic tests they needed to consider. Then there was amniocentesis and a battery of blood tests to check for what Brad considered to be every possible worst-case scenario. He wondered whether that had been the part that gave Emily that wild-eyed doe in the headlights look. She'd said nothing else, though, as they headed down to the lab for the preliminary testing and blood and urine samples. That time, Brad had waited patiently in the waiting room.

Now, as he watched her rolling out a pie crust, he filled a mug of coffee and knew he needed to get out and check the herd, take a minute with Cliff, his foreman, and tackle all the hundreds of other chores that needed to be done to keep this ranch up and running—but he didn't. He stood there, watching Emily.

"You don't need to stand over me and watch me like that. I'm not going to fall over. I'm pregnant, and, God forbid, at my age, this isn't what I expected, but we'll have to tell the kids, and then you need to get the crib set up. I gave away most of the baby clothes, so we'll have to start over. Then there's your family. We'll have to tell them… and I don't think I'm comfortable having an amnio." She dropped the rolling pin on the counter, putting her hands on her hips as she looked up at Brad, appearing totally at her wits' end. The floor was covered with flour, and so was the front of her jeans and shirt. Her hair was pulled up in a messy bun, and she had a spot of flour on her cheek as she walked in a circle as if she couldn't figure out what to do.

"Emily, talk to me. You think I haven't noticed? From the moment the doctor told us you were pregnant and then how far along you are, you've had this look about you as if someone's yanked the carpet out from under you. You still do. No one said you had to have the amnio."

She shot him a look that was far from that of the reasonable wife he'd married. She made a noise before squeezing her eyes shut, resting her hand on her head, and groaning. "Maybe not, Brad, but did you hear all the tests he listed off and the importance of having them? Then he said I was old."

"He didn't say that, Em. Don't put words in his mouth," Brad added, wondering if every pregnancy was different, because he couldn't remember her being this off kilter when pregnant with Becky.

"He may not have come right out and said it, Brad, but he made his point clear. I'm no spring chicken. He made it sound as if I'm running out of time."

"That wasn't what he said, Em. He was talking statistics, and the chances of genetic problems, birth defects, and things going wrong has increased, but he stated a number of times that you're not fifty yet."

"As if that's the magic number," she snapped.

He took another swallow of coffee before setting his mug down and walking over to her, sliding his hands over her arms and down until she finally gave him her attention. "It's not the magic number. He was just giving facts is all, Emily. He also said you're in great health, that there's no reason to anticipate a problem, and do you remember what he also said?"

This time she actually rolled her eyes. "You mean to celebrate."

Brad slid his hand over her ass, pulling her closer and holding her to him. "Yeah, to celebrate." He leaned down, kissed her neck, and rubbed her nose with his, running his hand up her back and pulling her shirt free from the waistband of her jeans. He kissed her again. This time she was responding more, and he ran his hand up between them, touching her silky skin, slipping her bra up and running his hand over her breast and her nipple. She hissed and leaned her head back, pushing into him.

He loved her breasts, playing with them, taking time to touch and taste every inch of her. Then she was gripping his shirt, squeezing as she pulled him closer, kissing him back, tasting him, moving as if she couldn't get close enough to him. He had her backed up to the fridge, and he lifted her as she wrapped her legs around his waist, her arms around his neck, her tongue entwined with his. He was quickly losing his reasoning as he felt the heat and passion going from zero to two hundred in a matter of seconds.

"Dad!"

He nearly dropped Emily as he stepped back, but he couldn't turn around. He couldn't believe he hadn't heard the kids! Katy was behind them, and the door slapped shut, and he could hear Becky and Trevor come in. He was doing everything he could to pull himself together, and he glanced down at Emily, who was breathing hard, appearing dazed and unsteady. He called out over his shoulder, "Next time make some noise, Katy. Stop sneaking up on your mom and me."

She actually giggled, and he listened as the kids took off upstairs, chattering. He pulled Emily closer still, pressing a kiss to her swollen lips, his jeans tight, with no hope at this moment of easing his discomfort.

"You're leaving me like this, aren't you, unsatisfied and needing you? Damn you, Brad, for starting something you couldn't finish." She was leaning into him, fisting his shirt and breathing hard, obviously as frustrated as he was.

"Yeah, well, your kids' timing sucks," he said and kissed the top of her head.

"They're your kids, too," she said, moving against him, sliding her hands around to his butt and rubbing against him, which wasn't a good idea.

"Not when they interrupt us, they're not." He kissed

her again before stepping away, and of course she noticed his source of discomfort, as her eyes went right to the erection pressing against his jeans.

She smiled at him. "Tonight the kids are going to bed early, and so are we."

He had to step back again, as she was about to touch him, reach for him. She had that look of desire in her expression that he was feeling deep down. "You stay right there." He pointed at her, stepping back again, and then started out of the kitchen and outside, listening to Emily call out to the kids to help get supper ready and finish the pie.

All Brad could do was stand outside the house, taking a deep breath, wanting to snarl and growl as he started into the barn.

Chapter 6

Brad was wearing reading glasses, sitting in the living room with the paper. What was it about her husband that no matter what he wore or did, or even the older he got, the sexier he was? The man stole her breath at times like this. She left Katy and Trevor in the kitchen, packing up their lunch for school the next day, as she walked over to Brad. She reached up and undid the top two buttons on her shirt before standing between his legs. He didn't look up, so she set her hand over the paper and gently moved it away. His expression seemed amused as he slipped off his glasses, and she leaned over, resting her hands on the arm of the chair, giving him an eyeful of her cleavage.

"The kids are almost done making their lunch," she said, leaning closer and pressing her lips to his, loving the feel of kissing him. Maybe she'd taken it for granted how much she needed to kiss Brad and touch him, to be with him as much as she needed to breathe. She knew he appreciated the view.

"And where is our youngest?" He rested his hand on her waistline and slid it over her hip and over her rounded cheek. It made her want to straddle his lap, wrap her arms around his neck, and kiss him, taste him, feel every inch of him pressed against her and inside her.

"Upstairs, putting her pajamas on." She licked her lips, feeling herself warm as she pressed her butt into his hand.

Maybe he knew, as he said, "Uh-uh. Not here."

"Mom, we're done making lunch. Can we watch TV?"

"No TV tonight. You have school tomorrow. Upstairs, bedtime," Emily said over her shoulder rather sharply without taking her gaze off Brad. The heat in his expression let her know he was ready for her, ready to take her to bed.

"Seriously, Mom? It's only eight age. I'm not tired yet," Katy said just as the phone rang.

Emily wanted to weep as Brad stood up, his hand still on her, holding her. She slipped her hands into his shirt, gripping him, and she squeezed the material, pulling herself closer to him. He patted her butt and pressed a kiss to her cheek. "Not quite yet."

"Dad, it's Uncle Neil!" Katy called out just as Trevor came in and picked up the remote, flicked on the TV, and sat down.

Brad slipped his fingers to Emily's shirt buttons and did them back up, grinning at her. "G rated until we're upstairs," he whispered. "You get the kids to bed now while I talk to Neil." He strode away, taking the phone, and Emily took the remote from Trevor, flicked off the TV, and said, "Bed, now." She pointed to the stairs just as Becky bounced down in her pink housecoat. "You, too. Turn around, up to bed."

"Mom, seriously, it's too early," Katy said.

Becky added, "Can't we watch TV for a bit? We always get to."

"No, new rules. No TV. You guys have been way too tired in the morning. Off to bed now." She clapped her hands as she listened to the protests from the girls as they marched upstairs. Trevor had groaned only once when she'd turned the TV off, but now he was already gone and getting ready for bed. She glanced back at Brad, who was walking around in the kitchen, speaking with Neil and smiling at something he'd said.

She gestured to him, feeling the urgency and need. He winked at her as she walked closer to him, wanting to rip the phone from his hands, listening to the one-sided conversation.

"That's fantastic, Neil," Brad said.

She could hear Neil's deep voice coming through the phone and knew when the brothers were settling in for a long conversation. She stood in front of Brad and then crossed her arms. She was about to tap her foot.

"Neil, just hang on a second." Brad was watching her, and she couldn't believe the amused expression on his face as he pulled the phone away. "What are you doing?" He actually started to laugh at her.

"Just reminding you not to get lost. I know you and your brother can get talking for hours, and that's not happening—"

He leaned in before she could finish and pressed a kiss to her lips. "I'll be off by the time you get the kids settled. Go run a bath. I'll be right there," he said. He gave her a quick kiss again, running his hand over her hip, which had her wanting to reach up and slide her arms around his neck. "Go on."

He actually pulled away, stepped back, and patted her

ass again. His eyes were teasing, and his expression was both amused and distracted as he starting talking with Neil again, leaving Emily no choice but to walk away upstairs, make sure the kids were in bed, and wait for him.

Chapter 7

He hadn't meant to talk to Neil that long, but his brother had been excited about getting the resort back up and for some reason had figured he needed to report to Brad about how well the management team was working. The bottom line was great. There were a few more hurdles left to climb, but he and Candy were flying back in the morning with the kids, and Neil had set up the business side so he could run it from their home in Hoquiam, which was a short drive from the ranch.

Brad locked the doors and flicked off the lights before making his way up the stairs, listening to the sounds inside the house: the tick of the clock in the living room, the squeak of a bed from the kids' rooms. He glanced once to his closed bedroom door and went down the hall to look in on the kids. Trevor was already asleep in his double bed, his blue quilt pulled up and his hands resting on his chest. His room was neat and tidy, but then, when it came to keeping things in order, putting his clothes away, and making his bed, he never had to be asked. He just did it. That was the one thing Emily had to nag the girls about.

He peeked into Becky's room, beside Trevor's, where she too was fast asleep, her brown teddy bear tucked under the covers beside her. Their little girl was now a preteen and was growing up far too fast. He heard a sound from Katy's room at the end of the hall. Her door was shut, and he could see light spilling out. He tapped on the door.

"Katy," he said, then opened it when he heard the bed squeak as if she'd jumped in. She was pulling the covers up but had forgotten to close her laptop and the chat window from whoever she was talking with. Brad walked in and took in her wide eyes, the same color as her mother's. She knew she'd been caught. He stared at the screen and the teenage boy on the other side, dark hair, and said, "Time to say goodnight." He clicked off the screen and closed up the laptop.

"So who was that?" he asked, taking in her face. Katy was the spitting image of Emily. Although she was from Emily's first marriage, Brad had raised her as his own since she was a little girl and just talking.

"Steven," she said, pulling the covers up and covering her mouth. He knew she was hiding a grin.

"Come on, sit up." Brad gestured toward her. It was past time they talked with Katy about the boys and the time she was spending gabbing on FaceTime, Skype, and the phone.

She sat up, the covers going to her waist. She was wearing a sleeveless nightgown, white with blue flowers, very pretty. It was rounded at the neck, and he realized she'd been sitting in that thin gown as the boy gaped at her.

"Tell me about Steven. Who is he?" Brad crossed his arms, looking down at Katy, trying to see her as a horny teenage boy would. He found he wanted to pull at his shirt collar, because he wasn't liking what was happening right under his nose.

"He's a friend in my class. We were just talking."

Brad was nodding, at the same time realizing Katy was trying to pull one over on him. He knew evading when he heard it. "You mean he's one of the boys who's been calling for you. He ever show up here?" Brad asked, but then, he didn't think one had come to the door yet. She'd gone to school dances, out with friends…was this Steven one of them?

She actually rolled her eyes, and he felt the moment his back stiffened. She must have realized her faux pas, as her eyes widened.

"Don't do that. Do not disrespect me, Katy," he said. "You're almost sixteen years old, and you're very much my daughter, and I will not hesitate to ground you until you're twenty-one if you ever pull that on me again." He didn't yell, his voice was too calm for that, but he saw the moment she understood. "I asked you a question about Steven, and this business here, having your webcam on while you talk to this boy in your pajamas as if he's in your bedroom with you, that's not going to happen anymore."

"Steven called, and I answered. He's just a friend," she said again, giving him a hard-done-by look as she crossed her arms.

Brad stepped closer and looked down at his teenage girl, who was resembling a woman more and more every day. It was downright dangerous, and he now understood how some fathers wanted to lock their daughters up and throw away the key.

"Your mother and I haven't sat you down yet and had a frank talk with you about boys and the dating rules. I think it's long past time we laid some things out. You have a lot of boys calling, and not one of them has taken the time to stop by here and see you. What I see happening is a lot of sneaking around behind our backs." Brad rested his hands on the foot rail of the brass bed. "From now on, the computer isn't allowed in your room. It's out in the living room with us. No more chatting online. You want to talk to a boy, he's going to have to show himself at the front door and introduce himself."

Katy sat up so stiffly, gesturing wildly. "Are you kidding? We live way out here. They can't just come out. Dad, you're being too old fashioned. Everyone talks online now. You're going to ruin my social life. I won't have any friends."

He wanted to laugh at her dramatics, but then he realized she was serious. He just shook his head. "No, I'm putting my foot down, Katy. This Steven has interests other than just friendship, so don't think you can treat me like a fool. Your mother and I know way better than you. You think we weren't teenagers once? I was a teenage boy at one time. I know exactly what that kid's agenda is and what's going through his mind."

She flushed but was still staring at him as if thinking what else she could say. "Dad, I like Steven, and he asked me if I could go to a party with him this weekend. It's just a few of the kids from school at a friend's house."

Here we go, he thought, *the dating, the pawing at Katy.* He hoped they'd drilled some values into her. "No, hell no are you going to any party. You're too young, Katy. For one, if Steven wants to take you anywhere, he needs to show his face on my front doorstep and look me in the eye before I'll ever consider it. You let him put his hands on you?" He expected shock, outright denial, but she appeared uncomfortable, and he wasn't liking this. "Katy, you answer me. Your mom and I already talked with you about sex."

"Dad!" She shut her eyes, and he could imagine by her expression that she was mortified at this discussion, probably the same discomfort he'd had sitting with Jed and Neil when his parents had sat them down, planning to give the birds and bees talk to three horny teenage boys. They had been red faced, tongue tied, and it had probably been one of the most awkward moments of his teenage years—but better awkward and embarrassed than knocked up.

"Katy, I don't care how embarrassed you are. We're going to discuss this. We should have talked about this more. You haven't answered me."

"Okay, he kissed me." She opened her eyes and said it as if it wasn't a big deal.

Brad stood straight and actually rolled his head, feeling the tension build as he crossed his arms again, looking down on her sternly. "I want to know everything."

She gazed up at the ceiling, and Brad was sure she was getting ready to roll her eyes again. He waited, and finally she said, "He put his hand under my shirt, but I swear that's all."

Three, two, one. He was counting in his head, breathing in and out. Oh yeah, he'd be having a word or two with Steven about any thoughts he had of sweet talking Katy into doing anything else.

"Dad, I'm not lying. I know what you and Mom said, and I'm not stupid. I'm not about to get pregnant. I like Steven."

"Okay, but no parties, and no more Skype or online chatting. He can show his face at the door and talk to me. You tell him that. I expect him to show up and do this the right way, no more sneaking around." He'd be sure to put the fear of God into that boy and make him think twice about messing around with Katy. "And this"—Brad scooped up the laptop and unplugged it—"comes with me. Now go to sleep."

"Dad…" Katy said in a voice that sounded so much like that of a little girl who still needed him.

He stopped in the doorway, looking at her as she lay back down.

"Is Mom okay?"

"Your mom's fine, just a little tired," he said, looking down on Katy and knowing they had to sit the kids down and tell them the news that another baby was on the way.

"Dad?" she asked again when he went to turn off the light.

"Yes, Katy?" he said.

"You're not going to upset Steven, are you?"

"Katy, you'd better get used to it. Any boy who has any interest in you is going to learn real fast that there are a few rules he's going to follow, and one of them is that he's going to respect your mother, me, and you. That means he's going to show his face at the door, and I expect him to understand that if he crosses any lines with you, he'll wish he was never born."

"I'm never going to have a boyfriend!" she cried out as Brad gazed up to the ceiling and flicked off the light.

"Goodnight, Katy," he said, and he walked out of the room to his bedroom, where his wife was waiting in a very warm and welcoming bed.

Chapter 8

She could hear voices and then realized they were coming from downstairs. She sighed, opening her eyes and taking in the light. She was on her stomach, her arm out, and the spot beside her was empty. Brad was already up, and the kids were downstairs, too, being awfully quiet. A quick glance at the clock, and she realized it was now almost eight and time for them to be out the door for school. She should get up and at least make sure everyone was ready and packed. Why hadn't Brad woken her?

In fact, she'd waited for him in the bath, her eyes closing, and then had climbed out before slipping into bed. She must have fallen asleep. She was now feeling completely unsatisfied as the warm sheets shimmered over her bare skin. She rolled onto her back and listened to the squeak of the screen door, Brad talking to the kids and then saying goodbye. Then quiet. She didn't know why that comforted her, the peacefulness and then the sound of her husband's footsteps downstairs. Would he come up, or would he leave to take care of his ranch? She rubbed the sheet on his side of the bed.

The stairs squeaked, and she breathed again, feeling such contentedness now in a way she couldn't explain as she waited for him to open the door. He was dressed in blue jeans and a black T-shirt, his boots on.

"You're awake," he said, stepping closer, holding a mug of coffee as he stood over her and took a swallow.

"You didn't wake me," she replied. She saw how his gaze took in all of her, knowing she was wearing nothing underneath. She moved her leg, and his expression changed to one of amusement and something else. She wondered for a moment whether he was going to deny her again. Maybe he had too much to do. She reached over and slid the back of her hand over his pillow.

"You were tired and out cold," he said. "There wasn't a chance I was waking you up last night, and the kids are old enough to get themselves ready and out the door in the morning. They don't have to have you down there organizing them," he said.

Yes, but they were her children, and they needed her as much as she needed them. Being there was just another way of saying how much she loved them. He frowned, maybe because of the expression on her face. Right now, she was stuck between wanting to stay in bed and feeling bad for not being up for her kids.

"You fell asleep on me last night. By the time I got in here, you were fast asleep. It was rather disappointing." He took another sip of coffee before sitting on the bed, holding out the mug, and Emily sat up and pulled her knees in, pushing back her long hair, which had to be a terrible mess. She reached for the mug and took a sip. It was still warm and tasted so good.

She allowed the sheet to slip down and felt his hand

skim the side of her breast. His gaze never left her. "I waited for you. You talked to your brother too long," she added.

"Hmm, maybe, but I needed to talk with Katy, as well."

Well, that had her attention. She sat up a little straighter, and he sighed, pulling his hand away. "You talked to Katy about what?" she said. What was going on with her daughter? She was about to throw back the covers and leap out of bed, but Brad must have realized, as he reached forward, setting his mug down and then resting both hands on either side of her, sliding them over her arms, holding her here. He was so close to her and was shaking his head.

"Stop panicking. I just checked on the kids before going to bed, and Katy had her light on still. Caught her on that damn computer, live chatting with some boy in her skimpy nightgown."

How come she'd missed this? When had Katy started chatting online in her room? "What happened? I didn't know she was doing that." She was missing too much. She should've gotten up this morning. She was always up with the kids.

Brad reached over and touched the skin between her eyebrows. "You're frowning and worrying. This isn't about something you missed or didn't do. This is about a teenage girl, ours, who's interested in boys. If you've taken a look at her lately, she's going to have many of them dogging her heels. We've talked with her about sex, but we need to sit her down and have a more direct talk. I did some of it last night."

Well, now she was worrying. Brad was all about his family and being in charge, and sometimes he handled things in a tough way that made it seem like he was laying down the law. At times he didn't even tell her.

"What talk did you have?" she said. "What did you say, and why?"

His thumb was rubbing circles down her arm, and then he sat up, glancing away for a second as if he needed to think. "I took away her computer. From now on, house rules are that she goes on it downstairs where we are, where we can watch over her. No more chatting online with boys. Told her this Steven needs to show his face at my door. I plan on having a word with that boy."

She just stared at Brad. She knew that any teenage boy who showed up looking for Katy would be met with Brad pulling him aside and most likely scaring the crap out of him. Katy would be angry, and Emily couldn't help being torn. Sometimes things needed to be handled tactfully, which wasn't a word in her husband's vocabulary.

"She was in her pajamas, a thin nighty, talking with the webcam on so this boy could see everything," Brad said. "She needs to understand, despite her innocence and how young she is, that boy is looking for a lot more right now and will do and say anything to get it—and I'm not about to let that happen." He dropped his hand away and leaned back, taking her in. She could see the guard dog inside Brad now that rarely took time off. It was a part of him that was always there, lurking somewhere in the background.

"Don't push so hard that Katy backs away, Brad. She turns to her dad now, too, and even though she doesn't see him often, I don't want her running to him because she feels she's got no voice here." She touched Brad when she knew he was going to interrupt her. She could see the moment they were no longer on the same page. "She's a young lady, a teenager, and I know her friends are dating. She's told me she wants to date, Brad, and it's time we let her. I don't want her thinking we don't trust her, or she could start rebelling and sneaking around. I don't want her to ever become sneaky. Her dad…"

"I'm her dad, Em," Brad said, cutting her off rather sharply. "When does Bob ever put any real time into seeing her? Once in a while doesn't cut it. Maybe he sees her a handful of times a year."

She hadn't meant for Brad to think Katy wasn't his responsibility, because she was. It was hard blending families when there was an ex in the picture. They'd just had the guardianship papers drawn up, though, and Katy was now Brad's. He had a say. If something happened, it wouldn't be Bob stepping in—it would be him. "Of course she's yours. Bad choice of words, but Bob isn't going away. He made that clear when he agreed to let you have guardianship. You already know Katy sees you as her dad." Emily reached for Brad again because she sensed she'd said something that could divide this family. And they were a family.

"Em, I'm either her dad who she answers to or I'm not, but you know damn well that a family can't work when there's an outside power source."

"I know that, and it's not what I'm saying." She wanted to bang her head against the wall at this complicated situation she was creating. "Bob has always lurked in the shadows, you know that. He loves Katy, but she will always come second. You've always been her dad, ever since we moved in here, ever since she was a little girl. I'm just saying that Bob has always been about throwing a monkey wrench into a situation, any good situation, so no one can be happy. I don't want Katy realizing that she has an ally there in Bob. If we're all of a sudden restricting her and making it so difficult for her to be a teenager, she could run to him."

"I'm not bending on this, Em. She *is* a teenager." He gestured sharply with the flat of his hand as if the discussion was over and he'd already decided what was going to happen.

How was she going to get him to understand that with teenagers, it was different? Their hormones were running wild, and they didn't reason like adults. "Brad, on this, you may have to bend a bit. I don't want Katy sneaking around." *Or sneaking off to Bob,* she thought, *calling him and playing up how Brad and Emily are the big bad parents.* She couldn't take that.

"Em, give me a little more credit, would you?" Brad sounded genuinely hurt.

He stood up, and of course there was a distance between them now. All the flirty teasing that had been there a moment before was now gone. He was mad, not understanding what she was saying. She truly was making a mess out of this.

"I love you, Brad, but sometimes you can be so difficult. You're not understanding teenage girls."

"And you don't have a clue about teenage boys," he snapped right back at her, the fire blazing in his eyes telling her that she'd said too much and pushed too far. "There's only one thing on a horny teenage boy's mind, and that's how he can find a way to get Katy alone to feel her up. Ultimately, all he's looking for is how to score. That's it. All he wants is the prize, not the girl, and once he has it, he'll toss her away and move on. Is that what you want for Katy?" He was being crude and mean, and of course she didn't want that. Of course she didn't want to see her daughter crushed.

"Give Katy a little credit, Brad. She's smart, and yes,

she is a little boy crazy, but you've taught her well. She knows and understands values."

"Are you sure about that, Em? Because what I saw was a girl playing at being a woman, but she's too naive to figure out all that it entails. She is going to get burned. She needs stronger boundaries right now."

She wanted to argue, but then, what did she really understand about teenage boys? She frowned up at her husband. Was he seeing something she was missing with Katy? She'd been distracted lately, and for a moment she felt her children slipping through her fingers.

"I need to take care of the stock." He sighed, and she could see in that moment how he was pulling away, his hands on his hips, his coffee forgotten as he turned and went to the door.

"Brad," she called to him, and he stopped and turned as she pulled her knees higher, wrapping her arms around her legs, "don't be mad at me."

"I'm not mad, Em, but sometimes, with Katy, I'm starting to think we're not on the same page," he said. Then he left, his footsteps creaking on the stairs, and with him went a little piece of her heart.

Chapter 9

Brad tossed a bale of hay onto a stack in the large corner of the barn where it had been stacked since he could remember. He loved the smell of freshly cut hay and could always tell when mold took hold. That had happened in the last batch, which had become damp near the bottom. It always happened at this time of year, when they were finishing off the winter stock. He stopped and took a breath, swiping his arm across his forehead, his hands sweating under his work gloves.

He felt a hand on his back, skimming up, and he whipped around to see his wife standing before him, watching him with an expression filled with so much, from needing him to being upset.

"I didn't hear you come in. Everything okay?" he asked, taking in her hair, which appeared freshly brushed and was hanging loose down her back. He noticed now how much longer it was, as she usually kept it tied back or pulled up in a messy bun. Her jeans were low riders and made her ass so round and eye catching, and she had on a sleeveless shirt, low cut with snaps for buttons, hugging all her curves. She was standing there, looking up at him as she reached up and undid her top button, showing off the cut of her cleavage.

He knew he had raised an eyebrow, as she licked her lips. He wanted to laugh at her, as this was the second time she had all but tossed herself at him. He couldn't remember her being this kind of temptress.

"I need you," she said, stepping into him, touching him as she slid her hand around his waist and over his butt. She pulled him closer and leaned her head back as if waiting for him to kiss her, to take her.

"What is going on with you?" He pulled off his gloves and tossed them down on a bale of hay before sliding his hand to her cheek and into her hair. She shut her eyes, leaning into him.

"These damn pregnancy hormones," she said. "I want —I need to have sex. All I can do is think of you, and I want you so damn much it's driving me crazy. It's all I can think about." She was gripping his shirtfront, and he was loving the fact that his wife was all over him. He looked at her and leaned down to kiss her before glancing over his shoulder to the open barn door, where anyone could walk by and see them.

"Why don't you let me finish up here, and then I'll come in and we'll take a break?" he said, then kissed her again.

"No, here, now." She slid her hands over his shoulders and was pressing right into him on her tiptoes, reaching up to kiss him. She wasn't slowing down as she started undoing the buttons on his shirt. She was over the edge and wasn't about to be stopped, and even he had to admit that being out here where they could be caught at any moment added something to the sex.

He pulled her back into a stall that had been cleaned

out and backed her against the wall, pulling at the snaps of her shirt, opening it and showing off her creamy lace bra. Her nipples were poking at him, and he slipped the bra up and over her full breasts. He lifted her, and her legs wrapped around his waist.

Her hands wouldn't stay still. They were running over his chest and lower, reaching between them to find his belt. She squirmed against him, kissing him hard and desperate as if she'd been drowning without his touch. He broke the kiss, but her mouth and lips went to his neck, his chin. "Em, holy God, slow down," he said, but she wasn't listening as she went for his lips again.

"Whoa! Geez, bad timing!" It was Neil, laughing.

Brad couldn't believe it as he stepped back, holding Em, unable to turn around. At the same time he was sure he heard Em whimper as she held on and then slowly unwrapped her legs from his waist, sliding down the front of him, feeling all his hardness. He wondered for a second whether she was trying to make him suffer.

"I didn't mean to disturb you two. I...Candy and I were at the house and looking for you. I came out here, and—wow, so sorry! I could just walk away, let you two finish what you were doing, pretend I didn't see anything." Neil actually started laughing again.

Brad was wondering why his brother was still standing there if he had plans to walk away. More like plans to make him suffer. Emily patted Brad's chest as she reached up and snapped her shirt closed, giving him a withering look, something he hadn't seen before on her face.

"Neil, your timing sucks," she said as she went to step around Brad, but he slid his arm out and stopped her before she could step away from him.

"We'll finish this later," he said in a low voice that did little to hide the agony he was in after his hot little wife had gotten him all worked up to the point that he'd expected relief but was now suffering again.

"You keep saying that," she said, looking far from happy as she stepped away from him. She said something to Neil before Brad could turn around, and it was no fun being caught at his age by his brother, the evidence of his arousal still evident in the discomfort of his jeans.

"Why don't I give you a minute?" Neil said. "I'll head to the house with Em."

Yeah, his brother knew. This time when Brad turned around, he stared at the empty barn and listened to Neil talking to his wife as they stepped out, but his wife wasn't talking back.

————————————————

Chapter 10

————————————————

She walked from the barn to the house in a daze, listening to Neil prattle on, about what she didn't have a clue. He reached for the back door and pulled it open before she could lift her hand. Instead she fisted it and looked over at her very attractive, charming dark-haired brother-in-law. This was the first time ever that she wasn't happy to see him.

Maybe he knew, because he said, "I'm sorry, Em. I can't believe what I interrupted. Maybe I should have walked away, but I was thinking more about giving my brother a hard time. That wasn't nice." He winced down at her. The teasing had disappeared, and he had picked up on her frustration. "Is everything okay?" he asked, touching her arm and glancing over his shoulder to the barn.

"Fine, it's just your timing really needs some work, Neil. It's as if I have to sneak around to have alone time with my husband, which isn't as easy as it looks." She gestured to the house, wondering whether she sounded as crazy to Neil as she did to her own ears. "Sorry…I seem to be putting my foot in my mouth today." She was snapping and being short, which wasn't like her.

"You're really upset with me," he said, and now she felt like crap, because the last thing she wanted was to make Neil feel bad.

"No, it's me. I'm upset with myself. I'm sorry, Neil. I'm overreacting and snapping at everyone, I think, or it feels like it. I said some things to Brad this morning and realized something came out the wrong way about Katy, about her dad. I just feel awful," she said, needing to apologize to Brad, hoping he'd forgive her. At the same time, she still wanted him to dial it back so Katy wouldn't start sneaking around, wouldn't feel the need to turn to Bob, who'd never been a part of her life in a meaningful way. Maybe she was just being paranoid.

Neil rested his hand on her shoulder, and she heard footsteps but didn't need to look to know Brad was coming. She did, though, start up the steps before glancing back and stumbling. She didn't know how. She felt hands on her, holding her, and then Brad lifted her into the house.

He put her down and snapped, "What the hell, Em?" He sounded mad even though he'd felt so good, but he let her go into the kitchen, where Candy was making herself at home, pouring Michael a cup of juice.

"Is everything all right?" Candy asked. She too appeared alarmed, looking past her, probably to Neil.

Emily rested her hand on Brad and glanced up at him, taking in his strength and his expression. It seemed he wanted some answers, too.

"Was dizzy. Must have turned too fast."

Brad reached for a chair, slid it out and around, and sat Emily down in it. "Stay there," he said. He sounded mad, and of course both Neil and Candy appeared puzzled.

Emily could see Cat in the doorway, all smiles, and she

couldn't help holding out her arms to the little girl Neil and Candy had adopted. "I love your hair today, and that dress," she said. Cat was dressed in a cute yellow dress with thick straps and a white sweater overtop, sneakers and white ankle socks on her feet. Her dark hair was held back by two gold butterfly barrettes on each side of her head, and the cochlear implant behind her ear was hidden by some of her longer hair, which was now past her shoulders.

"Do you want to tell them, or shall I?" Brad said to her when Emily just held Cat, looking down at the little girl, ignoring Brad and everyone else.

"We should tell the kids first," she said as she glanced up, taking in the curiosity in Neil's expression. Candy was frowning, staring straight at her as if she wanted to get Emily alone and have a heart to heart.

"Well, here they come," Neil said, glancing over his shoulder just as Emily heard the kids talking as they clambered into the house, making about as much noise as a herd of elephants.

"Mom, Trevor got hurt again," Becky called out as the back door banged, and there was a thunk as she dropped her backpack. Emily was out of her chair, but Brad and Neil were already at the back door when Trevor appeared with Katy. This time he was holding his arm.

"What happened?" She must have raised her voice as she put Cat down, because all she could feel was panic and worry and anger. Brad was questioning Katy, who was beside Trevor, and Neil didn't look too happy, either.

"It was Jason this time. He was sitting in the aisle seat on the bus, and he stuck his foot out. Trevor fell. He laughed. The bus driver caught him this time, but he yelled that it wasn't his fault, that it was an accident."

"It's okay, I'm fine," Trevor said. Neil was examining his arm.

"Looks like just a scrape is all. Has someone been hurting you, Trevor?" Neil asked, looking to Brad and then down at Katy. Emily was standing there with her hands on her face.

"I'm calling Jason's mother right now," Emily said. "It's time we have a word with that woman about the bully she's raising, who seems to think it's okay to hurt a special needs child." She was holding the phone and pulling open the drawer for the phone book when Brad took the phone from her and set it in the holder.

"Yeah, you're not phoning now," he said.

"Of course I am." Emily went to reach for the phone again, but Brad took it from the holder before she could grab it.

"No, you're not," he said a little louder. "Look, you pick up that phone and call the way you're feeling now, you're going to say something you'll regret."

"You mean because I'm irrational and not thinking clearly."

"Exactly."

She couldn't believe his high handedness. Instead of taking a breath, stepping back, and being the one to see reason, she wanted to yell. "That is so chauvinistic! So help me, Brad, if the next words out of your mouth are that because I'm pregnant, I'm not capable—"

"Whoa, you're pregnant?" Neil interrupted.

"What?" Katy said at the same time Candy reached for Emily, touching her back and rubbing it. "You're too old to have a baby, Mom," Katy said. She was really upset, and now Brad was staring up at the ceiling. Neil was wide eyed as if he found this amusing, and Trevor was frowning.

"Mom, you're having a baby?" Becky said. "That's so cool! Can I help change diapers and feed her?" She was excited and jumping around, and Emily touched her chest, not sure who to talk to first, because she was still stuck on Katy and the fact that she was horrified by her predicament.

"Katy, this isn't the end of the world," Brad said to her, sounding rather calm.

"It's worse. What are my friends going to say when they see my mom pregnant?"

Emily opened her mouth to say something, but the fact was that hearing Katy add her disappointment to what should have been a happy moment made her feel like crap. "Well, I'm sorry to disappoint you, Katy, but I'm not that old, and I'm having this baby."

"Mom, you're starting to have gray hair, and you, too, Dad."

"That's enough, Katy," Brad said. "You need to apologize to your mom, because you don't talk to her that way. We are a family, and this isn't about you. This is another brother or sister you're going to have, and your mom is far from old."

"Hey, let me be the first to congratulate you!" Neil stepped in, hugged Emily, and smacked Brad on the shoulder. "Big surprise, you two. This is great, adding another Friessen to the brood."

Emily glanced over to her daughter, who crossed her arms and shrugged before saying, "Sorry, Mom." Then she looked to Brad for approval as if she'd done what was needed. "Can I have my computer back now? I have homework I need to do."

"Yeah, take it," Emily said at the same time that Brad said, "No, it stays downstairs where we are."

Trevor was rummaging through the fridge, Becky had dragged Cat off to the living room, and Emily threw her hands in the air and walked out, stomping up the stairs.

Chapter 11

Brad didn't know what to say, what to do as he watched his wife acting far from the predictable, steady, levelheaded woman she was. Candy appeared uncomfortable, and she frowned and opened her mouth to say something but instead lifted Michael and said to Katy, "Here, Katy, do you think you can change Michael into a dry pair of pants? His bag is at the front door."

Katy only hesitated a second, but Brad could tell she was considering what attitude she could strum up and whether she could get away with saying no. To her credit, she stepped forward and took Michael, who was small for three, and now chatting away, happy to be in her arms.

"Trevor, get out of the fridge," Brad said, as Trevor was about to pull out the chicken and sit down to eat. "Go wash your hands and then unpack your lunch kit and backpack."

"Emily seems a little off," Candy said when they were finally alone. Brad pulled out a chair at the end of the table and sat down, hearing a door clicking closed upstairs.

"I can honestly say that being pregnant at this time in her life is throwing Emily off a lot. She's flying off the handle, overreacting…" He stopped because Neil and Candy exchanged a look that appeared amused.

"She sounds like a pregnant woman," Neil said.

"Hormones, Brad," Candy said. "Cut Emily some slack. I can only imagine having teenagers at this stage of her life. I think there's a time, too, though, when you're done with the diaper stage, and it can be a shock realizing you're going back to it."

Brad was staring at Candy. How did she know this? The way Emily had acted with Katy, he was still bothered. They'd never once had a serious disagreement over child-drearing before.

"Emily said something to me about Katy and her dad. What's that about?" Neil said. "And this teenager thing I'm seeing…" He gestured with his thumb to the living room, where all the kids seemed to be gathered.

This had been one area where he'd never expected to disagree with Emily or have an obstacle. "I caught Katy chatting online last night, her webcam on, with some boy. She was in her pajamas, her thin nightgown, which would have given that boy an eyeful. I laid the law down and took her computer away. It stays downstairs now so there's no chance she's sneaking on to it to chat up some boy at night in her room, period. Told her this boy needs to show his face at the door, too. I expect the kid to behave himself, and after I speak with him—"

"You mean scare the hell out of him," Neil said.

"You'd do the same thing, Neil. Just wait until Cat is a teenager and it's your turn."

"Don't be mean, Brad. I didn't say I disagree with you, just wondering whether you want me to show up, too, so this kid has to face both of us and understand it wouldn't be the smartest thing for him to cross any lines with Katy."

"Oh, you two, stop it, really!" Candy said. "I can imagine Emily would've gotten a little upset if you said that."

"She's a teenager, Candy. She's impressionable, with not a clue what boys want. They're both kids with raging hormones that will put them in a heap of trouble unless she understands our expectations clearly. The boy, too. She's going to take chances, and that boy is only thinking about how fast he can score and with who." Brad tapped the table, and Neil was nodding in agreement.

"So what does that have to do with Katy's dad? I thought he wasn't really in the picture," Candy said, looking to Neil and then Brad.

"Emily's suddenly worried that Katy's going to become a rebellious teenager if I don't ease up, or that she's suddenly going to run to Bob. It's the first time she's brought her ex up with regard to raising Katy. He doesn't have any role in that, though. I have guardianship now." Brad couldn't explain how much it bothered him that Em didn't trust him, as if she were saying Katy was her daughter, not his.

"You know what? I'm going to go up and talk to Emily." Candy gestured upstairs and then stopped in front of Neil. Her expression concerned Brad for a moment before she rose up on her tiptoes and pressed a kiss to his brother's lips.

Then she left, Neil watching her as the possessive husband he was. "You've got your hands full, Brad. What can we do to help?"

Before he could say a word, the phone rang. "Hold that thought," he replied as he reached for the phone, wondering what boy was calling for Katy now.

THERE WAS SOMETHING ABOUT HINDSIGHT. Emily wished she could go back and check her mouth. She fisted her hand as she lay face down on the bed, knowing she needed to get up and go down and start apologizing, but where to start? Maybe she should start making a list and keeping it close. She shut her eyes as she listened to the voices, and then there was a tap on the door.

"Emily, it's Candy. Can I come in?"

She rolled over on her back. "Sure, come in," she said softly but made no move to sit up.

She heard the door click open and then closed. Footsteps. Then Candy sat on the bed, looking down on her. "Congratulations," she said softly. She reached over and rubbed Emily's shoulder.

"So how much of a fool did I make of myself down there?"

Candy's eyes danced with amusement. "It was entertaining but understandable. You have a lot going on. Tell me, are you happy about the baby?"

The million-dollar question. She hadn't had time to really consider all the ramifications and what this meant for her and Brad. "I was just getting used to the idea that I had more free time and Brad and I would have all this alone time together. The kids are older and they don't need me watching over them all the time, but now I'm going to have one needing all my attention. Does that sound horrible?"

She couldn't look at Candy. It sounded harsh to her own ears, and she had to close her eyes for a minute.

"Give yourself a break, Emily. Even I can see you haven't had time to come to terms with it."

She breathed out a little harder than she'd meant,

relieved that Candy understood.

"I have to say, though, about the Katy thing," Candy said, "I've never known you to bring your ex into the picture or to worry that Brad is pushing too hard with the kids."

She wondered what Candy was getting at. She stared at her toffee-colored eyes, which were filled with such confidence. Candy, her sister-in-law whom she loved so much and couldn't imagine not being friends with, was questioning her judgment.

"Are you saying I'm wrong?" She didn't want Candy not to be on her side.

"I'm not criticizing you, Em, I wouldn't do that, but I can understand the feeling of being a parent to a child who isn't yours biologically. Having someone hint that you're not the only parent, that someone else has a voice…you should understand, with Trevor. You're his mom. What if Brad had said Crystal had some say with Trevor that you didn't."

That was hitting below the belt. They had been there once, and it ached in her heart, knowing she had done everything for Trevor, had raised him, and then Brad's ex-wife had walked back in, wanting a relationship with him. She couldn't answer. It was such a mess, one she had dug herself into.

"Didn't you get guardianship papers, both of you, for Trevor and Katy? So there is no question. Brad has always been Katy's dad. He loves her, and I've never once seen him see her as anything other than his daughter. You can't have two sets of standards in the house, Emily. You have to be united or she's going to walk all over you."

This time she turned her head to Candy. "I know that, I understand it. I just can't help feeling that Brad is pushing too hard with her right now."

Candy nodded, and her lips twitched. "Emily, there's one thing about Brad, Neil, Jed, even Andy. They push, each one of them, and God help any boy who comes to the door or tries to mess with their kids. You know this already. He's not going to ease up, and I think you're not giving Katy enough credit. One thing I've seen with Katy, with all your kids, is that Brad is everything to them—especially to Katy. She looks up to him, she respects him, and she's had no worries that other kids do. I've seen something in her. Even though I've never met your ex, only heard about him from Neil…" She took a breath, reaching down and rubbing Emily's arm as if thinking about how best to say something.

Emily couldn't help the way her stomach knotted, dreading what was coming. "Don't say it. I know. If I were still married to Bob and he were in the picture as her father, she wouldn't be doing as well as she is. He has no strong family values, and Brad and his brothers, they had such good role models. I know what you're saying."

Candy smiled and took on an odd look. "I'm just saying it wasn't that long ago that I was Katy's age. Looking back, I didn't have a role model. I was the parent in a lot of ways, but I've noticed that Katy has figured out Brad and your ex, the differences, recognizing the father she needs and has. Don't start questioning is all I'm saying. You have to stand united together or Katy will pick you apart. Besides, has she ever questioned Brad's authority or said he's not her father?"

Good question. If it had been anyone other than Candy asking, she wondered how she'd respond. "She loves Brad. She looks to him for everything like all the kids. Even when her dad calls or she goes to see him, she still turns to Brad as if knowing it's his permission, his okay, his guidance that she needs, not Bob's." She shut her eyes, wondering when she'd started worrying and creating problems that weren't real. "Maybe I'm going crazy. Being pregnant at my age is messing with me more than I'd like. I guess I can add this to the long list of apologies I'm going to have to make."

She heard the footsteps, as she would have known the sound of Brad anywhere. The door opened, and Candy slid around as Emily lifted her head. "Everything okay?" he asked, looking at her with a dark, brooding gaze. He was holding the door and, she noticed, the phone.

"Great, sorry," she added as she sat up. "What's up?" She gave Brad a smile, but she couldn't help feeling such a distance between them. Something was on his mind.

"Your doctor called. He wants you in tomorrow morning to run some more tests and go over something that showed up today." Maybe that was the look in Brad's eyes.

Emily immediately jumped into panic mode, believing there was a problem. "Something's wrong, something bad. I knew it. I had a feeling something wasn't right."

"Em, stop it. He never said that, and it could be nothing. If it was serious, he would have had you come right in. Don't start freaking out and worrying." He stepped right up to the bed, where he was almost touching her. Then he glanced down at Candy. "It's good you're here. You keep her calm. Neil's going to throw some steaks on for dinner."

Emily went to get up. "I didn't start anything. I didn't think to invite you and Neil to stay…"

"Stop it, we've got it," Brad said. "You stay here. The kids will help," he added before turning away and walking to the door. He stood there for a minute, and she wondered whether there was more before he stepped out and pulled the door closed behind him, leaving Candy and Emily alone.

Chapter 12

Emily had been in a much better mood during dinner, sitting around the table in the kitchen with Neil, Candy, and the kids. It had been light and fun, and he could tell that having Candy to talk to had helped somewhat even though Emily remained distant. After Brad went to lock up the house and turn off the lights before turning in for the night, he had walked into the bedroom to find Emily out cold again.

This morning, they were back at the doctor's after getting the kids off to school. Brad waited for Emily to climb out of the truck, resting his arm on the tailgate. He took in how she looked on this warm day, the sun bright. She was now unusually happy. She was wearing a pale blue T-shirt, cut low to show her cleavage, which seemed to have grown overnight. Her jeans rode low on her hips, and she'd stuck her bare feet in flats. She stopped in front of him and raised an eyebrow, maybe wondering where his thoughts were. Her hair was down again.

"First the doctor, but then we really have to speak with

the school and the parents of those two bullies." She stood in front of him, rattling off what needed to be done as if she was going through a to-do list.

"First things first, Em. Let's find out about the tests, and then I'll have a chat with those parents. You're in no frame of mind to be doing that." He touched her shoulder when he realized she was misunderstanding again and was likely to say something she shouldn't. "And don't put words in my mouth. You even said something last night about all the apologies you're going to have to make. You may want to ask yourself how long you want to make that list." He couldn't help the twitch of his lips, smiling at the thought of his wife having to tell him over and over how right he was. She glared up at him, clutching her purse, and then walked through the door he held open for her.

He jabbed the elevator button as she stood stiffly beside him. He couldn't resist touching her as he reached over, running his hand down and over her arm. The look she gave him, though, should have had him backing up. He couldn't remember seeing the fire burning in her eyes quite that way. He needed to ease up on her or this could be a volatile few months.

The doors opened, and Emily stepped in, not looking at him. "So why do you suppose the doctor wanted to see me? I don't remember this happening with Katy or Becky. They were both easy pregnancies. Do you think something showed up?" She turned to face him as the elevator moved up.

The elevator doors slid open, and he pressed his hand against her lower back. "Em, let's just wait and hear what the doctor has to say."

Thankfully, they didn't have to wait long. As soon as the nurse behind the desk saw them walk through the door, she waved to them and took them into the doctor's office, where they sat down and waited.

Brad slipped his arm over the back of Emily's chair beside him just as the door opened and the doctor walked in. He was dressed casually today, blue jeans and a maroon T-shirt, and he was holding a file.

"Hey, Brad, Emily, thanks for coming in on such short notice." Dr. Keys sat in his black mesh chair.

Brad was watching Emily and the freaked-out look she had, so he reached over and took her hand. She let out a breath that sounded like relief, and he tried to give her a reassuring smile.

"Did something show up that I should be concerned about?" Emily's voice was a little shaky, and she squeezed his hand.

Maybe the doctor noticed, as he looked up and over to them.

"Doc, you got my wife all worked up," Brad said. So was he, but for Emily's sake he wasn't going to lose it.

The doctor was looking at the file and papers, and the look on his face had Brad's own chest squeezing so much that he had to work a little harder to draw a breath. A horrible feeling settled in his stomach that maybe his wife was right.

"Okay, there's no easy way to say this, so I'm just going to. The blood tests I ordered have picked up some abnormalities, so we need to get an amnio scheduled." He tapped the desk with his fingers and then leaned back in his chair.

It was instinctive for Brad to wipe his face as he squeezed Emily's hand. He didn't need to look at her to see the fear of the worst-case scenario written all over her face.

"I don't understand what it is you're picking up," Emily said.

"Well, the amnio sample will tell us more, but I suspect this child could have neural deficits."

Brad couldn't say a word as he listened to Emily's sharp intake of breath. He blinked, trying to get one reasonable word to form in his brain. "I need plain English, please. Just what is it you picked up in a simple blood test?"

"Well, that's the thing. The test indicates there could be something. A neural deficit could be any kind of learning disorder, from down syndrome to something else, some genetic abnormality. Because your boy has autism, Brad, there's also a high likelihood that this baby could have autism, as well. It may not be a best-case scenario."

Emily pulled her hand away, and he watched as she rested both hands on her stomach. "But I'm not Trevor's biological mother," she stated as if she'd suddenly put a wall up to protect herself from all this. Brad couldn't help feeling as if somehow, she was blaming him.

He wasn't sure what to make of Emily's response. "So you're saying there's something wrong with this baby?" Brad was gesturing at Emily as he cleared his throat, leaning forward.

The doctor stared right at him. "No, I'm not saying that. With Emily's age, the blood test that came back showing something…"

"Could be nothing," Brad said, interrupting. He leaned forward and cut the air sharply with his hand. He didn't know why, but he was trying to force this doctor to take it back, to say nothing was wrong, that this was all a bad dream.

"Tests do show false positives all the time. All we know is that there could be something." The doctor flipped open his calendar. "That's why we need to get the amnio scheduled right now and test the fluid. Then we'll have some answers."

"No, it's too early. I could miscarry. The risks are too high." Emily was looking straight ahead, and then she stood up, holding her purse as if it held everything she owned.

"Em, sit down. Let's just listen to the doctor for a second." Brad went to reach for her hand. She'd never pulled away from him before, but this time she took a step back and was shaking her head.

"It's not too early," the doctor said. "Amnios are generally done between sixteen and eighteen weeks, and there are always risks, but it's riskier not to do the test. Take a day or two and think about it, but we need to schedule this to have some answers."

"Riskier for who?" Emily snapped.

The doctor's face became sympathetic for a moment as he watched her.

Brad felt this conversation heading down a one-way street to disaster. "What's the reason for the amnio? I need you to explain everything. Something could be wrong, and then what, you can fix it?"

"That's not what he's saying," Emily said without looking at Brad. If he didn't know her so well, he'd have believed she was strong, but her voice, the way her knuckles were clutching her purse so hard they were white, told him how scared she was. She had withdrawn as if she needed to protect her heart, and he couldn't remember her ever doing that before.

The doctor leaned forward, having become uncomfortable with the conversation, and said nothing as he glanced over to Brad. Maybe he expected him to settle his wife, talk some sense into her, but Brad didn't have a clue what the doctor was trying to say. His entire expression had taken on an awkwardness that pulled the knot tighter in Brad's chest.

"Sometimes, when we find out something's wrong, parents need to make hard choices," the doctor said. "They need to consider whether to bring a child into this world who's going to be severely disabled or have some medical condition that will reduce his or her quality of life and put a financial or emotional strain on the parents." He stopped talking, and Brad understood what he was saying.

"You're talking about terminating a pregnancy because a child's not quite right or is a financial burden." Brad gestured to the doctor, who this time glanced over to Emily and shook his head.

"I'm talking about choices, giving you, the parents, the choice once we have all the facts. You need to decide what you're able and willing to deal with, to handle. You have no idea the number of parents who may love their children but end up placing them in the system because they're unable to cope with the emotional and financial stress of caring for a child with atypical needs."

Emily was nodding, but it wasn't in understanding. She was holding herself so tight that Brad wondered, if he touched her, would she step back again?

"It must be so inconvenient that every baby isn't born perfect," she snapped at the doctor. "You don't know me very well to suggest I could turn my back on a child. You insult me."

Brad had never heard her speak to someone this way before. It was cold and impersonal, and he hoped she'd never come to speak with him that way. "Em, that's not what he's saying. He's just laying out options."

"Oh, I think he is. Let me ask you, if something bad were to show up, would you encourage me to abort?

Would you do everything within your power to convince me it would be the right thing to do?"

The doctor didn't say anything as he leaned back in his chair again. The tension in the room was thick.

"That's what I thought," she said, and without a glance over to Brad, she pulled open the office door and walked out.

Chapter 13

She'd never felt a distance between her and Brad, like a thick wall building higher and wider, more than now. No matter what they'd been through, they had always been able to talk—yes, yell at times, but they always found a way to get through things together. This was the first time Emily had ever felt this kind of loneliness.

Brad wasn't a woman. He was a man, with a man's body, and he couldn't carry a child. That was something she had been made for, to love and connect, to feel the child growing inside her, something a man could never understand. Because of that, she felt herself shutting down.

"I'm going to the school. When I get back, we need to sit down and talk," Brad said to her when he pulled up in front of the house to let her out.

It didn't matter that she'd wanted to go to the school. Brad had put his foot down and refused to discuss the matter of the school problems with Trevor any further. He felt that Emily holing up at home with her thoughts and agony was going to make a difference, but he had no idea what she was going through. So she said not a word as she pulled open the door, climbed out, and gave the door a shove closed before climbing the steps and hearing Brad drive away. She didn't turn around until he was down the driveway. Then she stood there, her throat aching and her eyes burning, wanting to curl up in a corner and just cry.

But she couldn't do that. She wouldn't do that.

Instead, she pulled open the door and lifted the keys to her minivan from the rack in the kitchen. She didn't bother taking off her shoes even though she knew she was tracking dirt. For some reason, she just didn't care.

She did reach for a sweater in the closet before leaving the house, pulling the door closed behind her. She didn't lock up before stepping off the bottom step and climbing into her vehicle. She started it and gave it only a second to warm up before backing up and pulling down the driveway.

She looked right and then left, wondering where to go, what to do. She didn't have a clue, so she just drove with no destination in mind. She flicked on the radio, flipping from one station to the other before grabbing the newest Adele CD and popping it in. She cranked it with the windows rolled up as "Hello" played. She loved the song, and she felt every word and emotion the singer conveyed. She sang as the music filled the vehicle, vibrating the speakers because she'd turned it up so high. Normally she wouldn't do such a thing, but she didn't care as she drove and sang, feeling only the music, the song, nothing else.

Chapter 14

The school wasn't going to take care of the bullying was what Brad took away from the meeting with the principal. He couldn't believe when the administrator indicated that he would look into matters at school, but nothing had been reported, and whatever happened on the bus would be addressed with the driver. To him, though, it sounded as if it had been taken care of. What stuck with Brad was the comment the principal made that some things were separate from school and needed to be dealt with by the community.

In other words, he wasn't about to do a damn thing, so Brad left the high school feeling as if he was going to have to take matters into his own hands. He really was glad Emily hadn't tagged along. He wondered when schools had started turning a blind eye to problems. Now, of course, he was starting to worry what they had been doing with Trevor if this was their attitude—just one more thing being piled on their plate.

When he pulled in at home, wondering how he was going to explain what had happened at the school in a way that wouldn't set Emily off, he realized the minivan was gone. As he stepped out of his pickup, he was pulling his cell phone from his pocket, but there was no message from Emily. Especially after what had happened that morning at the doctor, he expected Emily to let him know if she had to go out. He started to worry that something had happened.

Before he opened the door, he was dialing her cell, and it went right to voicemail. "Dammit, Emily, answer your phone. Did something happen? Where are you?" He left the message, willing her to call him back. He was inside the house, in the kitchen, looking for a note, a sign about where she'd gone, anything, but there was nothing out aside from the coffee mugs sitting in the sink where they had been left earlier. It appeared as if nothing had been touched.

He waited, and of course there was no call back, so he picked up the phone and dialed Neil.

"Hello?" Candy answered on the first ring.

"Hey, it's Brad. Listen, is my wife over there by any chance?"

"No, she's not. Is everything okay?" Candy asked.

No, of course it wasn't, but he didn't want to get into anything over the phone. "You know what? If you see her, ask her to call me. I'm kind of worried here," Brad said.

"Yeah, of course. Do you want to talk to Neil?"

He could hear his brother's voice in the background and shook his head even though he knew Candy wouldn't be able to see. "No, just call me if Emily shows up there." He hung up before his brother could get on the line or Candy could ask anything else. "Dammit, Emily, what the hell is going on?" he said to the empty house. He stared at the midday clock just as the back door was pulled open and a knock sounded.

"Hey, boss!" Cliff called out. "Charlie called about the

rotted shed where the feed is stored. His workmen can come today to replace the wall boards and seal it up. He said they'd be here in fifteen minutes, but I need to know what you want me to do with the bags of feed in there now." He had one booted foot in the door and was wearing a baseball cap and a sleeveless brown shirt. His jeans were a mess, covered in grime and dirt, but they always were, and his face had a day or two of growth, as it always did, as well.

Of all times for the contractor to have it together and be able to show up and get something done. Brad rubbed the back of his head as he went to the door and followed Cliff out. "I hadn't planned on him showing up so soon, but maybe it's just as well," Brad said as he walked with Cliff across the property, glancing once more at his silent phone, wondering where his wife was, what she was doing, and why she hadn't called him.

There was one thing he and Emily didn't do, and that was leave the other to worry. When she finally called or came home, Brad planned on sitting his wife down and having a heart to heart about the issue at hand, about the baby and her need to walk out on him without a note or a message of any kind. No, he'd been through this once before, and he planned to never go through it again.

Chapter 15

The winds were starting to pick up where she'd pulled over at a lookout after grabbing a muffin and hot tea at a bakery just outside Olympia. She just sat there, watching the trees as the wind blew in the late spring storm. The sky was gray and thick, with no break in the clouds. She had no idea how long she'd sat there behind the wheel, just letting the events of the day play out in her mind over and over. Her cell phone continued to ring repeatedly, and every time she saw Brad's name on the screen. He was worried. Of course he was worried, and probably angry because she'd left without a word to him.

She should call him, tell him she was okay, but every time she picked up the phone to dial, she pressed "End" before completing the call. She couldn't talk to him right now because she didn't know what to say about what she was doing. She had just driven without a destination in mind all the way to Olympia and then turned around after filling up the vehicle again. Now she was stopping for a break, just sitting and trying to figure out what she needed to do. She sipped her tea and rested, worried about what the doctor would find, that there was something wrong with the baby.

Would Brad want her to terminate? For the first time, she didn't want to know his answer, because every thought she was having about having this baby was about something being horribly wrong, about having one more obstacle to climb. She wondered what her breaking point would be, whether she wanted to have to deal with another challenge. She rested her head against the steering wheel.

The short blast of a siren had her jumping to look up as a state trooper pulled up behind her. She sat up straighter and set her cup back in the cup holder, watching the side mirror as the trooper got out and started walking to her window. She turned the key and rolled down the window as he approached.

He was of average height and a solid build, and he settled his hat on his head. He had shades on, so she couldn't see his eyes. "Everything all right, ma'am?" He was looking inside her vehicle at her and then into the backseat. His hand rested on top of the minivan.

She swallowed. What was it about law enforcement that always had her sweating? "I'm fine. I was just tired and pulled over for a minute to drink my tea."

He was staring at her in a way that was making her awfully nervous. "Can I see your license and registration, please?"

"Of course." She nearly jumped, tapping her forehead with her fingers while grabbing her purse. She pulled out her license and then reached in the glovebox for her registration. She handed both to the officer, sweating in her short-sleeved shirt, at the same time wanting to reach for her sweater in the passenger seat to slip it on. It was the cool wind blowing through her window.

"Stay here, I'll be right back," he said.

Emily wracked her brain, hoping there wasn't some outstanding ticket she'd forgotten to pay. She tilted her head to watch him as he sat in his car on his radio, maybe on his computer, too. She knew they had them in their vehicles. Her phone was ringing again, and she picked it up, seeing Brad's name flash on the screen just as the cop returned. He watched her watching the phone.

"Just my husband calling," she said, putting down the phone without answering.

He handed back her license and registration. "Ma'am, it's not a good idea to hang out here for long. Is everything all right?"

What could she say? *No, my picture-perfect life is falling apart faster than I can figure out what I need to do.* "Everything is fine, Officer." She forced a smile, but he slid his glasses down, his eyes light blue and questioning.

To prove her point, she fastened her seatbelt and started the minivan while the cop walked away. She took a breath, knowing her time was up as she pulled back onto the highway and headed home.

Chapter 16

"I don't know where she is. She's not answering her phone. Something has happened to my wife, and I want you to start looking for her. I already called the hospital. She's not there."

Brad was furious. He'd called Emily's cell phone at least a dozen times, and she hadn't picked up. Something was wrong, something had happened, and he was trying to explain to the local sheriff that his wife wasn't some flake who just took off, and he wasn't about to wait twenty-four hours for a search to start. He wanted—no, demanded it happen now. The sheriff's office apologized and said all they could do was keep an eye out for any accidents until twenty-four hours had passed. Then they'd take a statement. Then they'd start looking.

Brad was livid, and he finally hung up, about to toss the phone at the wall until he took in the panic in the eyes of his children. He was scaring them, and that was the last thing he wanted to do.

"Dad, what's going on? Where's Mom? When is she coming home?" Becky asked.

Katy was pale, her expression bordering on distress.

"Dad, where is Mom?" Trevor asked. Katy was still just looking to him to do something, anything.

"I don't know. I'm trying to find—"

There was a tap on the door, and his heart jumped into his throat as he heard the squeak and footsteps.

"Hello."

Disappointment nearly knocked him on his ass when he realized it was only Neil, dressed casually in blue jeans, a dark shirt, and a leather jacket. The sun was now going down, and Brad couldn't remember ever feeling this lost.

"Dad, I'm hungry," Trevor said. Of course, in the middle of all this mess, there was no dinner for the kids. Nothing had been started.

Neil walked in, taking in everything: the scene, the kids, their faces. "What's going on?" he asked as Becky raced to him and started crying.

"Mom's gone!" She wrapped her arms around his waist, and he held her tight, his expression grim.

"You still haven't heard from her?" he asked as he rubbed Becky's back and took in Trevor and Katy. Brad stepped forward, holding his arms out for them, and Katy leaned into him, her arm around his waist. Trevor just stood there, looking up at him.

"Dad, Mom will be home soon," Trevor said.

Brad wanted to have his positive attitude and hoped he was right, but Emily had never done anything like this before. He was panicking. Maybe she'd had car trouble and her phone had died, or she was off the road in an accident, hurt and unable to call him. His mind was going places he didn't want it to go, and he didn't know what to say to the kids, who wanted the same answers he did.

"I'm sure you're right, Trevor. Let's get some dinner

started in the meantime." He squeezed Katy and could feel her trembling. *Damn it to hell, Emily!* He was going to have a serious sit down with her for doing this to the kids. It was so selfish, but he was worried. Something was wrong. Something horrible had to have happened.

Maybe Neil understood where his thoughts were going, as he said, "Your dad's right. Dinner, I'll help. Come on, kids, let's have a look in the fridge and see what we can throw together." He set his hand on Brad's shoulder as the girls went to the fridge and started rummaging. Trevor was in the cupboard, pulling out plates.

"What's going on?" Neil asked in a low voice. Of course he was worried. Brad was beside himself.

"I've called Emily over and over, and it keeps going to voicemail. I called the sheriff, but they won't start looking until tomorrow. Something had to have happened, an accident, something…"

He heard a vehicle then. His chest squeezed, and his emotions felt all over the map as he started toward the door, but the kids were already racing. He heard Katy and Becky call out, racing down the steps outside. "Mom! It's Mom."

For a second, Brad let out a breath in relief just as anger he'd never felt before toward his wife took hold. "She'd better have a damn good excuse," he said to Neil.

"As your brother, who's made every mistake imaginable and said every stupid thing I wish I could take back, I suggest you don't overreact here. Hear her out before you yell and jump to any conclusions."

He could hear Emily talking but couldn't make out what she was saying as he walked to the door, Neil behind him. He just stood there, watching Emily herding the kids to the house, looking unhurt and just fine. He glanced over to the minivan, which seemed in the same condition as before Emily drove away. What the hell?

She looked up at him, and there was something there in her eyes that seemed to flinch, pull away. He knew evading, the look of a person who'd done something not quite right. He'd lived it before. He'd never expected to again.

"Where were you?" he snapped. "I called you countless times. Did your phone suddenly quit working?"

She flushed with her arms around Katy and Becky, who were watching him, wide eyed.

He was mad, and he felt Neil's hand in warning on his shoulder, but he shrugged it away because he didn't want to be touched. Brad stepped out the door, his hands on his hips, just watching her. She swallowed, and he had to shut his eyes, knowing his wife was avoiding him. What kind of bullshit was this?

"Hey, kids, let's give your mom and dad some space," Neil said. "Let's see what we can scrounge up for dinner for you." He actually stepped past Brad, extending his arm and holding out his hand to the girls while holding the door open so they could step in past him. He leveled a sharp look at Brad, one that wasn't about to get through to his sound reasoning. The way he was feeling, he was already way past the reasonable man he considered himself to be.

The door slapped closed, and he turned his head, listening to Neil with the kids as they walked further into the house. He could sense Emily standing on the stairs as if waiting for him to say or do something. When he turned back to her, he was swept up with what seemed like a brooding storm beginning to build inside him. It was bubbling, and he didn't think he'd be able to speak calmly to his wife.

"I'm sorry," she said.

He turned his head so sharply to her, staring down at her, wondering who she was. His Emily was honest and loyal and loving, and they'd been through hell and back together. "Imagine my surprise when I arrived home to find the minivan gone, you gone—no note, no message, no nothing. Answer one question for me: Did you ignore my calls?"

She didn't need to reply. It hurt just watching her expression, that of a woman who couldn't hide anything from him. She literally had tears in her eyes as if she realized now what she'd done. She slowly nodded. "I needed some space to think, to be alone," she said.

She was clutching her purse, holding it against her so tight. The distance between them was quickly becoming a thick wall that he wasn't eager to push through.

"So to hell with me, our children, all of us, leaving us to worry whether you're hurt, injured, lying on the side of the road somewhere we can't do a damn thing for you. That's cruel, Emily. Never would I have expected that from you."

Her face flushed again as she looked down. "I'm sorry, you're right. It was thoughtless. I didn't think you'd be worried…"

"Are you kidding me?" he yelled, cutting her off, and she jumped. Maybe he was scaring her, but right now he didn't care, and he fisted his hand, trying to dial it back when he heard the squeak of the door.

"Hey, you two." Neil stepped in between them, his expression taking both of them to task. "Cool it. Brad, maybe you should take a walk before you say something you can't take back."

"And why don't you butt the hell out, Neil?" he snapped.

"Don't get mad at Neil when it's me you're furious with!" Emily shouted back.

"Hey! This isn't solving anything, and the kids can hear both of you inside. Take this somewhere else, Emily, Brad," Neil said.

The door squeaked. "Mom, are you coming in?" Katy was standing in the doorway, her face pale and scared.

"Katy, go back inside," Brad said, done with the interruptions.

"Don't tell my daughter to go inside. Yes, Katy, I'll be in in a minute."

This time, he felt as if she'd slapped him. When he glanced to Neil, he could tell he had also picked up on what she'd insinuated.

"So now Katy's your daughter, not mine? What's going on with you, Emily? You're putting up this wall, dividing this family on whose child is whose."

She flushed again, loosening her grip on her purse. She appeared flustered as she lifted her hand up and rested it on her forehead. "That wasn't what I meant. I just don't want you taking out your anger on me with Katy."

"Just Katy, or all the kids?"

"Okay, enough, you two." Neil stepped in again. "Emily, go inside. You, cool off." He jabbed his finger at Brad.

Brad just stared at his wife as she walked around Neil into the house without a glance back to him. She was talking to the kids as if everything was fine, but it wasn't fine.

"Don't go there." Neil jabbed his finger at him. "It may be best if I take the kids, all of them, back to my place. They can sleep over, and you and Emily can work through what you need to."

Brad knew he was well over the edge, but of course it

was a reasonable request, so he did the only thing he could think of. "Fine, take them," he said as he walked down the steps and over to the barn. He'd check on the stock and do what needed to be done, then head back to the house for a one on one with Emily. Maybe Neil was right. Having the kids gone would be better, considering his mood and the headspace Emily was slipping into.

Chapter 17

"Hey, you guys, guess what? You're coming for a sleepover tonight. Go pack a bag," Neil said to the kids as they crowded around Emily in the kitchen. She was slicing the leftover roast from the fridge, about to make sandwiches for dinner.

"It's a school night, Neil. That's not possible, not tonight," she said.

"Go," Neil said to the kids as if he hadn't heard her or wasn't about to listen to her. The kids appeared confused, Katy most of all. They were looking to her and then Neil as if they didn't know who to listen to.

Neil finally sighed and said, "Give me and your mom a minute, guys."

The kids all left the kitchen this time as Neil stepped closer to her, his hands on his hips, sliding his jacket back. "What is going on with you?" he asked, all his usual teasing and lightness gone. She half expected him to lecture her, by the way he appeared. This was a side of him she didn't like very much.

"I have a lot to figure out," she said, not wanting to talk

or apologize any more, considering she hadn't figured a damn thing out while driving. The only thing that had happened was that she'd felt freer with time and space, not having to decide anything. She had liked it. She fisted her hands as they rested on the counter. "The kids need to eat, Neil. They have school tomorrow. Tonight isn't a good night to take them."

"I disagree. The way you and my brother were going at it out there in front of the kids, both of you saying things you shouldn't be saying…this is a time bomb right here, right now, and the kids shouldn't be around it. Whatever is going on with you, both you and my brother need to talk, Emily." He tapped the counter with his fingers as if this was a done deal.

She was tired of everyone telling her what to do, and it was beginning to feel as if she were being dictated to again. She took a step away from the counter and took a breath. "You know what, Neil—"

"Stop it!" he shouted at her before she could say one more word. He'd never done that to her before, and she jumped, so startled it hurt. "Just knock it off, because you aren't being reasonable. I'm taking the kids, and you and my brother can talk. Let me give you some advice. There's a line you can't cross without going too far, and you're toeing it, Emily. Don't say one more word." He leaned in, his expression filled with an unforgiving hardness she'd never seen before.

All she could do was stare at him as he stepped out of the kitchen and said something to the kids. She listened to the pounding on the stairs as she went back to slicing meat and ignoring Neil, who was now standing there, watching her.

Chapter 18

Brad found Emily sitting at the kitchen table with a plate of sandwiches wrapped in plastic and an empty plate, waiting for him. Her hands were folded in front of her as he stopped in the doorway and just watched her watching him.

"I made you sandwiches." She gestured nervously and then held her chin up to him, waiting to see what he'd say. He was hungry, but he didn't think he could eat a thing, considering the distance between them. He'd never have believed in a million years this could happen to them. He did feel somewhat calmer, though, from the time he'd spent outside.

He didn't say a word as he walked into the kitchen and washed the grime from his hands, noticing a few strands of hay on his shirt from the bales he had been stacking. He took a minute to pull them off and walked over to the garbage to lift the lid and toss them in. Emily had slid around in her chair and was looking over to him, and he could see how wound up she was. The fact was that he didn't know what to say to her and felt himself slipping back into a fury as he thought of her callous remarks. For a minute, he'd wanted to strangle her—not literally, but to shake her at least.

"Am I in for the silent treatment all night?" she asked.

He considered walking out of the kitchen until he could gather himself into a better frame of mind, but he didn't. He took a step toward the table and then another before pulling out a chair and sitting down. It was his spot at the end, and she was there to his right, where she always sat. She did unfold the plastic and shoved the plate toward him before clasping her hands in front of her again tightly.

"Explain to me how you could be so thoughtless," he said before reaching for a sandwich and taking a bite.

She flinched as if she'd had time to think, to consider what she'd done. "I'm sorry. Maybe if I say it a few more times you'll hear me. I didn't stop and think about how you'd be feeling. I was only thinking of myself. I needed some space and a minute, and…" She stopped talking as if she had to think about was she was doing.

He swallowed and ran his tongue over his teeth. "So you were thinking of yourself, just you. You couldn't even be bothered to phone me and leave a message that you were okay, that you needed a moment to yourself. That was too much for you?"

"I…" She swallowed, and he could tell she was thinking. Maybe that wasn't such a good thing, considering where her thoughts had been lately.

"You what, Em?" he prompted her as she stared down at her hands and then back to him.

"All I can keep saying is that I'm sorry. I just didn't want to talk. I'd had the rug ripped out from under me, and I needed to think through some things, come to some decisions."

He dropped the sandwich in his hand back to the plate.

"Really, just you? I was in that doctor's office, too. This isn't all about you, Emily. This is you and me and a decision we need to make together. When was it that you decided you're alone and only you have to figure this out?" He leaned forward.

"Well, for one, Brad, it's my body. I'm carrying this baby, and ultimately it comes down to my decision."

He pounded his fist onto the table, and she jumped. He scraped back his chair, standing up so fast it tipped over. "You, just you!" He stepped away, looking down on her, and then leaned down to put his hands on the table.

She glanced up at him. "Didn't you do the same thing, dropping me off and heading to the school to address Trevor's problems because I'm not his mother, I don't have a say, and you're deciding everything?"

He couldn't believe she would think that. He stood over her, holding his hand up. "Stop!" He could feel the tension in the room skyrocket. "Do yourself a favor and don't say another word. You know damn well I've never done that. You are Trevor's mother. I went to the school to handle a volatile situation because of the stress you're under, not wanting to add to it. There's a big difference, baby, between what I did and what you did. I'm starting to get it, because you've already hinted a few times at the division in this family, between me and Katy. You're separating all of us. Katy's yours, Trevor's mine—and Becky, where does she fall?" He couldn't remember ever being this furious with Emily. Through all the heartache, they'd stumbled, but they'd always been able to talk, to reason. Right now, he didn't like who she was. He started out of the kitchen.

"Brad, you're twisting everything I'm saying."

He turned back to her in the doorway, and for a moment there was a flicker of something familiar in her eyes. "Don't start lying to me as well, Emily. Let's just leave it at this and say goodnight. I can't talk to you right now. I don't want to talk to you because I don't like you very much right now."

This time he turned away and started up the stairs into their bedroom, grabbing clean clothes for the next day before stepping into Trevor's room and setting them on the dresser. He listened to Emily's footsteps, and the door to their bedroom softly closed.

Chapter 19

The sound of the screen door slapping roused Emily from a deep sleep. She groaned, not wanting to open her eyes as a breeze fluttered in the open window. She could hear Brad outside, talking to someone.

The fact was that she'd tossed and turned most of the night, unsure of when she'd finally fallen asleep. Her conscience, which had been working overtime, had kicked in, bringing an ache to her heart. She'd eventually cried into her pillow, believing she was the worst person ever: a horrible mother, a horrible wife.

She once again wished she could go back and undo her choices, because now she'd have called Brad and left a message so he wouldn't worry. How could she have ignored all his calls? That was something Crystal would have done, his selfish, self-absorbed bitch of an ex-wife. She'd just stepped into the same arena, following in the same footsteps as only a shallow person could do.

The phone rang beside the bed, and Emily reached over, seeing Neil's number on the screen. She squeezed her eyes shut for a second as a wave of mortification flooded through her for how she'd acted with Neil, which had made him promptly reprimand her like a spoiled child. "Hello?" She winced, still wanting to hide out and not talk to anyone.

"Hi, Emily, it's Candy. How are you this morning?" She sounded so nice and kind. Emily didn't deserve it.

She sighed and lifted her hand but couldn't get her tongue to move.

"That good, huh?" Candy said. "Listen, I didn't want to bother you, but Katy forgot her English book on her desk, and apparently she really needs it today. Neil was going to swing by and grab it and take it to her at school, but I offered to call first."

Of course she had. Who wouldn't, after the shit storm that had happened, which she was responsible for. Emily couldn't blame anyone for needing to steer clear of her.

"I need to get up anyways. I'll take her book to school and drop it off for her," Emily said as she sat up, hearing a tractor start in the distance.

"Okay, listen, if you need to talk…"

"You know what?" Emily jumped in when Candy paused. She wasn't feeling the need to talk to anyone right now about what a screw up she was and all the bad choices she was making. "Thanks for the offer, but I just need some space, okay?" She didn't wait for Candy to say anything before she hung up.

Bitch! she yelled at herself as she pushed back the covers. "What is wrong with me?" She dropped her face into her hands for a moment, wanting to crawl back into bed and pull the covers over her head, but instead she made herself get up, wash her face, brush her teeth, tie her hair back, and get dressed. She tiptoed down the stairs, her heart pounding, as she feared running into Brad. At the same time, she felt the great big hole caused by her and now the wedge between them.

If she was honest with herself, she and she alone was the only one responsible for this mess. Was she going crazy? She was starting to wonder and worry about what would slip out of her mouth next. She forced herself to grab a granola bar after she swallowed a glass of water, then raced up the stairs to Katy's room. She took in the white bed, the covers strewn everywhere. Emily could make it for her, and she started to when she realized Brad wouldn't like it. He didn't like her waiting on the kids like she did. So she did her best to ignore the mess as she stepped over clothes from days past scattered on the floor to the dresser with the English book.

Emily snatched it up and then took in the papers scattered on the desk. There lay a photo strip from one of those photo booths that showed her daughter and some boy kissing. *Oh, shit!*

She couldn't believe what she was seeing, and for a minute she found her knees weakening. She lowered herself to the bed and glanced over to the door, feeling like such a fool. Here she was, accusing Brad of being too hard on her daughter, when she was the idiot. She set the photo on the book and carried it downstairs. She put it on the kitchen table, which was neat and tidy. If Brad had eaten, he had cleaned up after himself. She just stared at the photo, unsure of what to do, when she heard someone coming. The back door squeaked open, and she listened to Brad's footsteps thudding with the beat of her heart. She swallowed, feeling embarrassed and uncomfortable, and she found herself just staring up at Brad when he stopped in the doorway with a distant look in his eyes, watching her. He didn't say a word, but then, enough had been said. What could the man possibly say to reason with her?

She forced a smile to her lips and then let it fade when he narrowed his eyes as if trying to figure her out. "You sleep okay?" she asked, not knowing what else to say as she stood there, feeling his scrutiny. Never once since being married had this kind of hurt and separation existed between them. It was unsettling. This was a lonely place to be.

He inclined his head. He wasn't making this easy. Her heart ached as she searched and pleaded in that moment for her sound reasoning to return and fill her with some words of wisdom, something she could say to fix everything she'd done.

"I'm afraid you were right," she said as she held up the photo.

His shrewd gaze didn't go right to it. Instead, he took his time as he just stared. His eyes were frosty and distant as if he was trying to figure out what would come out of her mouth next. Then he stepped closer, his gaze dropping to the photo as he took it from her. He just stood there for a moment. His eyes widened, his nose flared, but, to his credit, he wasn't flying off the handle like she had. He was thinking. She always could tell by the way he stood, one hand on his hip, so focused.

"Who is this with her?" he asked, looking over to her.

She had to shake her head. She started to say, "I don't know," feeling for a moment as if she didn't know what was going on with her daughter at all. Maybe this was one more thing she'd screwed up.

She swallowed again when he sighed and tossed the photo down on the table. For the first time, she didn't have a clue what he was thinking. She wanted to reach out and touch him, but she wondered whether he'd step away. The thought alone had her wanting to weep. She'd done her best to damage things between them, so instead she wrapped her arms around her middle and waited for him to say something, do something.

"What do you want to do?" she asked him, knowing she wanted to grab hold of her daughter and shake her, yell at her, ground her.

He glanced down at Emily again, and she could see the anger for her still simmering below the surface. "Sit her down," he said. "Time to have that talk with her, or is this where you tell me I'm overstepping again and Katy is your daughter?"

She deserved that. She knew she did, even though knowing that didn't make it hurt any less. She just nodded, firmed her lips, and picked up her purse and the book, then stepped around Brad and lifted the minivan keys from the rack.

"Where are you going?" he demanded. This was a road she'd never expected to travel down, not with Brad. How quickly things were going from a love that could conquer all to a gulf so wide she could feel the damage between them. When had they gotten here?

Her throat ached as she cleared it, and without turning around, she said, "Candy phoned. Katy forgot her English book. I'm going to drop it off at school." She squeezed the heavy book, and for a moment she wondered what he'd say, but he said nothing as he walked away. She turned her head to see where he was. His back to her at the back door, he hesitated for an instant before pushing it open and walking out. Instead of feeling that they'd resolved anything, she couldn't help feeling they were further apart.

Chapter 20

The sea of wildflowers in the field beside the school lightened her heart. After dropping off Katy's book without waiting around to see her face, she was engulfed with this awful feeling of wanting to hide and not talk to anyone. It was easier, because avoiding everyone meant she wouldn't have to apologize for one more idiotic thing that came out of her mouth. She was drowning in fear, but she couldn't exactly single out what she was afraid of, because it was everything. It all came down to an unknown she couldn't picture, a loss of hope she'd never once felt in her life.

As it stood, she was leaving a trail of destruction with everyone, damaging every good relationship she had, because of what? She couldn't for the life of her figure it out. That she was lost was all she had come up with, confused, thrown a curve ball she didn't know how to begin to understand.

As she pulled up to the gate at Neil and Candy's and it slowly opened, she felt her courage slipping. For a second, she considered running, throwing her van in reverse and backing up. Her hand was there on the gearshift when Neil stepped around the corner and spotted her. He didn't wave as he normally would, just stood there, waiting for her to make a move. He was carrying a two by four over his shoulder. She was forced to drive in, her foot trembling on the pedal, her stomach in absolute knots.

She parked and tried to give herself a split second talking to, a second to pull it together before Neil appeared at her door. He didn't give her that chance, as he opened her door before she could do a damn thing. Now she was flustered, feeling heat in her face as she reached down and unfastened her seatbelt before slipping out and forcing a smile to her lips, one that fell far from her heart.

"Emily, this is a surprise." He was being polite as he held her door, but the teasing, welcoming spark for her that had always existed in Neil's eyes had left. Had she done that, as well? Of course she had, driving everyone away, pushing so hard, hurting everyone until every last person in her corner would flee. For the first time ever, she understood Brad's ex-wife in a way she'd never wanted to.

"I'm sorry," she said, standing in front of him, looking up at him, his neat and tidy appearance traded for a pair of faded blue jeans and a light shirt. He hadn't shaved today, she could tell, and he had a pencil stuck behind his ear. He glanced over her head as if thinking of what to say, then back to her, his expression softening.

"Did you make up with my brother?" he asked. She wished she could tell him that she'd done that, but the problem was that she didn't know how to begin to repair the damage she'd caused. It was appalling, the destruction she'd wrought in a very short time with every thoughtless comment, every action.

"I don't know how." Her voice cracked, and she felt

tears burn just as Neil pulled her into his arms and hugged her.

"Oh, boy, you sure made a mess of things, didn't you, Emily?" He rubbed her back, and when she pulled away, wiping at her face, the tears that lingered, sniffing loudly, he reached over and squeezed her shoulder before looping his arm around her. "Why don't you come on in and tell us what's going on?"

She couldn't move, though, because then she'd have to apologize to Candy, too, and right now she needed a second to figure out what to say. "I was rude to Candy. I don't know what's the matter with me, Neil. I've said and done so many stupid things since..." Since she'd realized she was pregnant.

"You scared Brad and the kids. It was thoughtless, what you did yesterday, acting like a spoiled teenager, but I think you know that," he said in way she knew wasn't meant to be cruel. He was direct at times and cut right to the heart of the matter. She wasn't sure she appreciated that right now, though.

"I just needed some space to think because I was so angry. I didn't want to talk to Brad or have him tell me how to think or feel or tell me what he thinks I have to do."

He was looking at her now as if he didn't know what she was talking about. Of course he didn't. Brad obviously hadn't told him.

"The doctor had us come in yesterday. Something showed up on the first blood tests, and now he wants to schedule an amniocentesis to find out what's wrong."

Neil just stared at her as if he wasn't understanding the problem.

"He suspects some neurological problem or something bad."

This time Neil's expression softened with understanding. "And you're scared."

She shrugged. "It's more than that. I reacted badly, and when he brought up autism because Brad had fathered Trevor, I realized that genetically, it's a possibility. For a second, I was angry at Brad and blamed him." She shut her eyes, because she hadn't even admitted that to herself.

When she opened her eyes again, she expected to see condemnation for her callousness, but instead there was sympathy. "That's not good. Do you blame Brad?" he asked. It took her a minute to realize he was serious.

"No, of course not. It was a reaction, actually an over-reaction. I'm finding I'm jumping all over the place lately, saying things I can't believe are coming out of my mouth. It's as if this crazy person has invaded my head and is making me think and say and do things I would never in a million years do. Brad, the way he looks at me now, I wonder if he hates me. I can't blame him." She had to press her hand to her stomach, to the tightness she felt building that made her feel so cold and alone even though it was another warm day on this first of June.

His hand rubbed her shoulder, and she looked up to the Neil she'd always been able to talk to staring down at her. "Oh, Emily, I had no idea you were feeling this way. Have you told Brad?"

Her throat was tight and dry. She wanted to weep at the coldness she'd seen in her husband's eyes. "No, he won't listen. I don't know how to tell him, to explain. I was such a bitch last night, Neil, and I'm never like that, ever. What if something is really wrong with the baby?" she cried out. "I don't think I want to know."

Neil put his arm around her, pulling her against him and starting to walk her to the house. "Come on. I think you're panicking about something before it's happened.

The problem is that you can't see the road ahead, and it's scaring the hell out of you, by the sounds of it. The thing is, Emily, none of us can, so stop freaking out. Get the amnio, the results, and then deal with it. But you have to talk to Brad, tell him, and work through this with him. This isn't your decision to make alone."

She stopped walking and just breathed, then looked up to Neil, wondering whether she should tell him everything. He'd be angry, and she still couldn't believe she'd said it. She knew he'd ask about it anyway. "I told Brad it was my body and he wouldn't understand. I don't want the amnio, and he can't make me have it. I pretty much said to Brad that this was my decision. Can you blame him now for hating me?" she asked, taking in his shock. For the first time ever, she'd left Neil speechless.

Then the door opened, and Candy, her sister-in-law and friend, took in the sight of her falling apart with Neil. All Emily could do was burst into tears again and say, "I'm sorry."

Chapter 21

He'd never once gone to meet the school bus as it dropped off the kids, but out of everything that was piling up and testing his family, leaving him feeling as if he was slowly losing control, meeting the bus and addressing the two bullies seemed a simple thing to do.

He crossed his arms as he waited for the bus. When the door popped open, Brad stepped up, taking in the lady driving the bus. She had short hair that was almost black and a round face, an older woman, a little on the plump side. He stepped in on the first step and said, "I'm Brad Friessen. You have my kids on here, and my son, Trevor, has been getting picked on?"

The bus driver frowned and said, "Those two in the back, Deanna Miller and Jason Cresswell. I had a talk with them and mentioned it to the school." She said nothing else, which told Brad the school had already known anyway and wasn't about to address any part of this.

"Hi, Dad, you've never come to the bus stop before," Becky said, followed by Katy, who had such sad eyes. Trevor followed. Brad stepped down and let the kids out.

"First time for everything," he said. "Hey, Katy, where are Jason and Deanna sitting?" he asked, stepping back into the bus.

It was the bus driver who glanced up in the rearview mirror and said, "Fifth row, on the right."

"You talk to their parents?" Brad asked.

She shrugged. "Not my place. That was why I mentioned it to the school."

He nodded as he took another step in and looked down the aisle to where the culprits were sitting, both wide eyed. "Deanna, Jason, I'm Trevor's dad. He's the one you tripped."

Deanna actually opened her mouth, but nothing came out. Jason was wide eyed, with the kind of scared look kids got when they knew they were busted.

"You have a problem with Trevor?" he asked the kids, looking at both of them, knowing all eyes were on him from every child on that bus.

"No, sir," Deanna said, shaking her head.

"That's good. Listen up, if there's any more trouble on the bus and I hear you've been tripping Trevor again or saying anything you shouldn't, I'll be talking to your parents, understand?"

They both stared. If he'd had a parent call him out at that age, he'd have been crapping his pants. He turned to the bus driver then and said, "Any more trouble, let me know."

He stepped off the bus, hoping at least that this would be the end of those kids picking on Trevor. If it wasn't, the next stop would be to reach out to the parents. One thing he realized was that he wanted the kids to stop hurting and picking on Trevor not because their parents told them to but because they understood they'd gone too far. The last thing he wanted was for this to escalate into kids sneaking around, and even though he didn't know the parents, he suspected them getting in trouble at home could make them become sneakier with hurting his son. Sometimes, when things came from a stranger, children tended to listen just a little bit more.

Trevor and Becky had already started walking and were halfway up the driveway. Katy was standing and waiting for him. Her hair was pulled back, and she was wearing her tight skinny jeans and a shirt that was cut a little too low, the one he knew Emily never let her wear to school. With everything he had to address and fix and deal with, this could be just one more thing added to a very long list. He put his arm around her and started walking.

"So how was your day at school?" he asked, mainly to get a sense of how she was doing.

"It was okay. Dad?" She looked up at him, and he could see the worry she'd never had in her expression before. It was there in the way she leaned against him, in the tension of her arm as she held on to him.

"Yeah?" He didn't say anything else, just taking a minute with a child he felt deep in his bones was his own.

"Are you and Mom okay? Are you getting divorced?" She sounded so worried, that kind of fear kids could never hide.

Whoa, he hadn't been expecting that. He stopped and turned, putting both his hands on her shoulders and holding her there, looking down at her. "No, we aren't getting divorced. Your mom and I are just having some issues, some adult stuff, but we're working through it."

She was staring at him as if she didn't quite believe him. "Dad, I've never seen you and Mom fight like that before, and I don't want you to leave or Mom to leave or for you not to be my dad anymore."

Brad felt bad now for what had happened. He was still

angry at Emily—how could he not be after everything she'd said and done?—but he was thankful now that the kids hadn't seen everything. He was so glad Neil and Candy were back from Cancun, that he'd shown up when he had.

"No one's leaving. Sometimes adults make mistakes, too, Katy, and say and do things we shouldn't. Your mom and I are just working through some things." He squeezed her shoulder just a bit. "Everything will be fine," he added, hoping he was right, at the same time needing to make sure the kids didn't pick up on anything else.

She leaned in closer and hugged him. "I love you, Dad," she said, and in that moment, as he stood with Katy, he knew in his heart that Emily was wrong. Katy was his as much as Trevor was hers. They were a family, and for anyone or anything to come between them would tear them all apart. They may have fought and disagreed, but Katy would never turn away from him and run to Bob, thinking she could play one parent against another. She may have been a teenager looking to test boundaries, but she looked to him to keep her safe.

"I love you too, Katy, and I want to talk to you about something," he said as they started walking again, her arm around his waist, his around her shoulder. She glanced up at him with an expression that told him she knew she was about to be in trouble again. At the same time, he knew she was looking to him for everything. She said nothing. "Your mom found something in your room, a photo of you with a boy."

She winced, and her face colored. For the first time, he found himself remembering back to those teenage days, doing similar things, and worse. He just needed to make sure Katy didn't start sneaking around.

"Is the boy in the picture Steven?" he asked her, and she stared up at him as they walked together.

"Yeah. Am I grounded?"

He had to stop himself from smiling at her before shaking his head. "No, but you're not sneaking around with that boy." He wanted to know when she'd found time to sneak off and have the photo done, but he realized he was going to have to bend a bit and get Katy to bring this boy over sooner rather than later. "Is he the first boy you've kissed?" He hoped she'd say yes, because he was fast treading into new territory.

"Yes, but that's all, Dad. I promise. I told you before that we didn't do anything else."

There was something about the way she said it that made him believe her, but the boy…the more opportunities he got to be alone with her, the more he'd be working her down. Time to put a stop to that.

"He's your boyfriend?" He didn't want her growing up this fast. He wanted to bubble wrap her and keep all those boys far, far away from her.

"Would it be okay if he is?"

Well, at least she was asking him. He had to give her that, even though his first instinct was to say no, hell no. He cleared his throat roughly. "Tell you what. This boyfriend thing has rules, Katy. You're not quite sixteen. You want to see him, it's here." He pointed to the ground. "You invite this boy over. He can sit at the table with all of us, have dinner with us. He sees you here, do you understand? You're not sneaking off to be alone with him. Then we'll talk about you dating him, when you can go out and where. Understand?" He could see her thinking, frowning for a second, but not once did he see her consider arguing with him. For the life of him, he didn't understand where Emily was digging all these doubts up from.

"What if he doesn't want to see me then?"

He wanted to laugh as he looked up, then realized as he noted the worry in her expression that she was serious. "Hey, if there's one thing I know, Katy, this kid would be a fool if he didn't want to get to know you. Don't sell yourself short. You're honest, have a great head on your shoulders—with values," he added, hoping the last part sunk in for her. She was still looking at him as if he didn't get it, though. "If he doesn't, then you have your answer, Katy. Do you really want to date someone who has no respect for you, for us, who wouldn't come and meet your family?" He wondered what she'd say. He hoped she understood after all these years what family was all about.

"Okay, I'll ask him to come over," she said, and he couldn't explain the relief. It was as if a storm had passed him by, leaving him to weave through a path of destruction, but one by one, he was finally making a dent in the cleanup.

He realized he'd just tackled the easy stuff, though. What he needed to do yet was to fix things with Emily, with the baby…he had no idea where to start. Because of the hurt and betrayal he hadn't realized he still carried, he was now seeing Emily in a way that didn't bode well for them.

He just hoped, for the kids' sake, they could figure out where to go from here.

Chapter 22

Candy had set a blanket over Emily's legs as she curled up in the big round cuddler chair. Its deep burgundy was a great color in the open and welcoming living room. Emily loved Candy and Neil's house. Although smaller than hers, it really was a nice place.

Her eyes burned as she sat there alone, hearing Candy in the kitchen, where Neil had gone to make tea and pulled his wife with him. Maybe they were trying to figure out how to deal with her, how to talk to her, since no one had a clue how to reason with someone rocking on the brink of insanity. That was all she could think of to explain her jumbled emotions and her judgment, which had once been sound.

She clutched a Kleenex in her hand, dabbing at another tear that had leaked from eyes she knew were red rimmed and swollen. Being the messy crier she was, she knew that when she cried, which thankfully wasn't often, her entire face would be a swollen, blotchy mess.

Maybe that was why a sympathetic expression came

over Candy's face as she walked in with two steaming mugs and handed one to Emily.

"Thank you," she croaked out. She glanced around then at the quietness. "Where are the kids?" she asked. She didn't miss the smile that lit up Candy's face.

"Cat started school! I know it's late for her and late in the school year, but the elementary school called, and they had someone with experience with deafness. Today was her first day. It's exciting and scary. Neil took her in after dropping off all the kids. He said she was happy with the other kids, and she let him leave."

Neil walked in, carrying a hot steaming mug—coffee, she could smell it from where she was sitting, and for the first time she wanted to turn her nose up at the odor.

"I just put down Michael for a nap. He was so tired," Candy said as she leaned against Neil. He lifted his arm and put it around her shoulders where she leaned against him, pulling her legs up. He kissed her head, and the connection between them was so deep. It made her heart ache because it was a closeness she needed, one she'd damaged with Brad.

"I'm sorry to be such a mess. I wouldn't blame you if you don't want to talk to me." She took in the exchanged glance between Neil and Candy.

"Emily, you need to stop this, this pity party you're having. It's unbecoming," Neil said, his expression telling her he'd had enough. She was humiliated and felt her face warm. "Oh, stop it, Emily. All these years you've been a part of this family, I've never seen this side of you. We all behave badly at least once, and, being family, we'll forgive it as long as it's not a new side of you. Remember, this is your one time."

For a minute, she thought he was serious. Then she noticed Candy elbow him and shake her head.

"Emily, I just don't know what to say to make you feel better, to help," Candy said. "You are right about one thing. The way you're acting with everyone, pushing us away one minute and then making us walk on eggshells around you because we don't know what you'll do or say… what's wrong?"

Neil was rubbing his thumb up and down Candy's arm. "She and Brad had disturbing news about the baby," he said in a low voice.

She had to shut her eyes to the sympathy in Candy's expression for her. Of course she'd understand better than anyone. After losing her baby the way she had, as well as any chance of having children with Neil, she'd suffered the worst fate. Maybe she was being selfish.

Just then, there was babbling over the monitor. Michael was waking up.

"I'll get him," Neil said, then glanced at his watch. "I have to go pick up Cat at school, too. I'll take him with me." He was up and taking the stairs two at a time, and she could hear the way he spoke to his son. He loved him so much. If there was one thing about Brad and his brothers, even Andy, they loved their children, their families, their wives. It was such a powerful thing to be loved by them.

Candy smiled, reached over, and turned off the monitor as if the man fussing over his son was a private moment they shouldn't be listening in on. "So what happened?" Candy asked. "Is it true what Neil said? Is something wrong with the baby?"

The million-dollar question. "You were there when the doctor called, when Brad came up and said the doctor wanted to see me. Apparently something had showed up on the blood test."

Candy shrugged and then shook her head. "What was it?"

"Well, that's the thing. We're not really sure. It was some abnormality, the doctor said, so he wants to schedule an amnio now, but I don't want one, and I'm feeling pressured." In that second, she took in what she'd said. They didn't know anything, they didn't have an answer. So why was she acting as if the worst thing possible had happened when it was far from that?

Candy appeared confused. "I'm not sure I understand, then."

"Oh, I'm making a mess of this, aren't I?" Emily took a sip of her tea, staring into the amber liquid, hoping for some divine intervention. "I insinuated to Brad that this is my body and my decision. I can't believe I said that, but I just open my mouth lately and stuff flies out. I just wanted space to think, to consider, because I have never in my life felt as if everything is out of my control. It's like…" She glanced over to Candy, and then there was Neil, carrying Michael, watching her.

"But that's the thing, Emily," Neil said. "It's not just your body. This is your husband, too, and the two of you are together. You decide together. The moment it becomes just you or just him, your marriage is over." He glanced once at Candy and then leaned down while holding Michael. "I've gotta go," he said. His lips were close to Candy, and he just watched her, studying her as something passed between them. Then he kissed her tenderly before pulling away, grabbing his keys at the door, and walking out.

Emily listened to the door close and was left there alone with Candy, with her thoughts and what Neil had said.

"He's right to a point, you know," Candy said. "It's

your body, but you're having this baby together, and you need to talk to Brad about this decision. You know Neil and I have been through this. He blamed me for a long time when I lost the baby, after the hysterectomy. If I'd just told him I wasn't feeling well…I've beat myself up a hundred times, if not more. If I could just go back…" She looked up with such a haunted look. "But I can't. We've moved past it, but it's always there, that memory, as if to remind us of a time that we almost destroyed each other. You and Brad," she said, gesturing between them, as she seemed to need a minute to pull her thoughts together, "you're two people I look up to: what you have together, what you've done, the love you have, the love in your family, and how you have each other's backs. Don't let yourself go down that road where you think you need to figure it out yourself. Go home and talk to Brad, tell him how you feel. You need to stop shutting him out. He needs you as much as you need him." She let the silence linger for a moment, giving Emily time to let her words sink in.

"Okay, I'll try," Emily said, lifting the blanket off her legs and putting her feet on the floor.

"And, Emily?"

She glanced over to Candy, taking in the seriousness in her expression.

"If you find your mouth is about to take over and you're going to say something stupid and unforgivable, stop talking."

As Emily took in that last bit of advice, she realized it was the most important of anything she'd heard. She just hoped she could find a way to follow it and take a minute before her mouth ran away on her.

Chapter 23

Katy had just walked into the house when Brad heard a vehicle. He was expecting Emily, but again she seemed to have disappeared. It took only a second to realize it was Neil pulling in. He started down the steps as his brother climbed out and lifted Cat from her car seat and Michael from his.

"The kids home?" Neil asked.

"Inside." He gestured behind him as Cat walked up the steps, smiling broadly up at him. "Hey there, you." He reached down and lifted her, giving her a kiss on the cheek. "Katy and Becky are inside. Why don't you go find them?" He held open the door for Cat as she walked in.

"Emily's at our house," Neil said. The way he said it, Brad knew there was more, and it probably wasn't a good idea to be talking around the kids.

"Hey, Katy!" Brad called out.

"Yeah, Dad?" she said. He could hear the moment Becky and Cat found each other, as the giggles and chatter started.

"Come take Michael and watch him for Neil, please."

Katy walked to the door and reached for Michael, who went right to her arms. Brad also knew, the moment Neil saw what she was wearing, that his brother was obviously on the same page as him.

"Thanks, Katy," Neil said. He waited until he heard her walking into the house, then raised an eyebrow and frowned. "Uh, she had a sweater on this morning…"

"Yeah, I know." Brad gestured behind him. "Today is about picking my battles. Already had the boy talk with her, so I'm going to overlook the outfit for now. What's up?" he asked, stepping over to the railing and leaning against it.

"Oh, I'd say I've never quite seen Emily falling apart before. She showed up to apologize, and I'm afraid I laid into her a bit. She explained what the doctor said, how she overreacted."

Brad rubbed the back of his head and neck. "Yeah, well, in my opinion the doctor didn't handle things very well. He was leaning toward finding out so a decision could be made, and he feels we should consider terminating if something is wrong with the baby. I saw the tailspin that sent Emily into." He scraped his booted foot on the rail, still feeling raw from what Emily had said.

"I see, I didn't know that. Is that what you want?" Neil asked.

"I'll tell you what I want, Neil. I want my reasonable wife back, not the craziness that seems to have taken over her. She told me it was her body, her say. This is the first time I've felt as if we're on two separate paths, and I don't know how to get back to where we were. Any decision about the baby needs to be discussed between both of us. How does she not get that?"

Neil didn't say anything as he crossed his arms over his

faded T-shirt, staring out as if this was a problem he didn't have an answer for.

"You know how I feel about family, Neil. I thought Emily was on the same page. That's what sucks about all this. I feel as if somewhere along the way, I lost her, or she pulled away. I don't know how to reach her and pull her back." He glanced over to Neil before he heard a vehicle. Emily drove in and parked beside Neil's light SUV.

"Well, if you want my advice, don't let her walk away. She's scared, and she knows she screwed up and said things she shouldn't have and didn't mean. You may have to grow a thicker skin for the next little bit until Emily can find her footing again."

"And if that doesn't work?" Brad asked as Emily climbed out of the vehicle, started around the back, and seemed to hesitate.

"Since when did you ever need help talking to your wife? I'm sure you can think of something." He reached over and jabbed Brad's shoulder playfully with his fist before he pulled open the door and walked into the house, leaving Brad and Emily alone.

Chapter 24

She was terrified as she stood in front of the only man she had ever truly loved, the love of her life. She was wondering at what point that had left the equation. During everything, all their struggles, it always had come down to the fact that they had each other.

"I was thinking I should start a list, write down everything I need to apologize for, every thoughtless remark or cruel thing I've done. Or can I just try to say I'm sorry again? For the first time, I swear, I don't think I'm thinking clearly. I love you, and I can't believe I became so selfish and mean and…"

Brad reached for her hand and pulled her closer, holding her hand. She wanted to sag with relief, but then the tears came, and she scrunched her face as she walked into him and his arms went around her, holding her.

"Hey, what's going on in that head of yours?" he said, holding her so close for the first time in days. Where before she felt as if she'd been left floundering, now she was being pulled in to shore. She'd been so lonely, a loneliness she'd created.

"I need you. I didn't mean to tell you that you don't have any say. I was just scared, and I lashed out. I wish I could just take it back." She sniffed loudly, wiping her face on his faded blue shirt, her tears creating one big wet spot.

Then she looked up at him, resting her chin on his broad chest, and his hands went to her face, brushing her hair back, just looking at her and taking her in. She felt herself tear up again because his expression had softened. At the same time, she was grateful he was looking at her without the hate he had earlier. Just thinking of it made her ache.

"Please don't hate me anymore."

"Oh, stop it, Emily. I never hated you. I love you, I just didn't like the way you acted very much is all. You can't run and push me away because you're scared. We have to talk together, okay?"

She nodded, having a hard time catching her breath.

The door squeaked open behind them, and she didn't want to turn around and let anyone see she'd been crying.

"I'm going to take the kids again," Neil said. "I told them to pack more clothes to spend the night, and you two can work things out."

She nodded, feeling Brad's arms around her. It was a safety net she appreciated right now. "Sounds like a plan."

"Hi, Mom. Bye, Mom," Katy, Becky, and Trevor said, and everyone stepped out at once.

She cleared her throat and took a breath. "Have fun," she managed to get out as she watched her kids climb into Neil's SUV and took in the shirt Katy was wearing. She started to pull away and even lifted her hand.

"Don't," Brad said to her.

"Brad, she's not allowed to wear that shirt to school. She knows that," Emily said, wanting to call Katy back.

"We'll deal with it later, but Katy and I have already settled the Steven issue. He's coming for dinner."

Emily looked up at Brad, wondering what he was talking about. "What?" was all she could think of saying.

"Katy is my daughter. She knows that. She has a good head on her shoulders, but she's testing her boundaries right now, and we just had a talk so she understands. She's growing up, so I've had to shift some things around for her. Steven will come over here, see her here, no more sneaking around."

As Emily watched Neil back out, Katy rolled down the passenger window and waved, calling out, "Bye, Mom! Bye, Dad!" Her daughter had a bright smile, happy and part of a family who would always love her, always look out for her.

This time, when she might have put her foot in her mouth and said something she shouldn't have, she instead remembered Candy's words of wisdom and kept her mouth shut.

Chapter 25

He stepped into the bathroom, taking in Emily lounging in the bathtub. Her eyes were closed, but she wasn't asleep. It seemed, for the first time since she had found out she was pregnant, as if a sense of peace had come over her.

Her eyes opened, and she just watched him with that heavy-lidded look she got when she wanted him. At the same time, he could see something there. She was worried he'd walk out the door.

Ever so slowly, she lifted her hand from the sudsy water, reaching out to him. She didn't say a word, and nor did he as he undressed and climbed in the bath, facing her. She slid her legs on top of him as he slid his feet around her. He rubbed her foot and squeezed, and she took a deep breath as she leaned her head back against the rim of the tub.

"Oh, that feels so good, Brad."

He kissed the side of her foot as he lifted her leg and ran his hand over the soft skin and up her thigh. She hissed and ran the back of her hand over her mouth as she gasped.

"Don't tease me," she said. She moved forward, straddling him and settling onto his lap. Her lips went to his as she slid her arms around his shoulders. Her breasts, which he loved to play with, pressed into his chest.

He ran his hand over the soft skin of her curved bottom, feeling the roundness of it and then where she was ready for him. She was kissing him deeply, her tongue touching his, tasting him, and she moved closer.

He'd have slowed her down and teased her if this were another time, but not tonight. She rose up and settled down on him, taking him deep inside her, and he pulled her down until she'd taken all of him. He just held her there, her eyes wide, filled with so much emotion and love that he just wanted this moment to feel her while buried inside her.

Then he allowed her to move.

"Oh, Brad, I need you so much," she cried out as he felt her coming apart around him, but he wasn't done, he was far from done. He lifted her from the bathtub, water splashing, and set her down on the floor. He grabbed the towel and dried her quickly and then himself before lifting her and taking her to the bed, where he laid her on her back and stepped between her thighs, entering her hard and fast so she squeaked and trembled.

She reached for him, trying to pull him down on top of her, but instead he climbed on the bed on his knees and draped her legs over his thighs as he moved inside her faster, holding her tight so she couldn't move and was forced to take all of him over and over.

When she screamed out, his own shout followed as he filled her with his seed again. He collapsed on top of her, and for the life of him he didn't think he could move.

"Wow, that was…wow." She breathed out, running her hands over his back, holding him to her.

He grunted, which was the only reasonable sound he could manage to get his brain to strum up. He couldn't speak—not yet, anyway.

She was tracing circles on his back, up and around, before kissing the top of his head. "I keep thinking of what the doctor said about a problem…"

He pulled out and rolled over onto his back, then pulled her against him. Her leg instinctively went over his, her hand to his chest, as if she knew how she fit against him. "'Possible' is what he said, not for sure. There are false positives, and he knows nothing for a fact until an amnio is done. We're at step one. Don't jump all the way to a hundred. There are answers we haven't even gotten yet, so how about we stop with the what-ifs and worst-case scenarios?" He hadn't meant for it to come out so harsh. He felt her flinch and held her tight when he knew she'd pull away. "Stop overthinking, because that's the problem between us," he said, pressing a kiss to her forehead, feeling her settle in.

"Okay. I get it, I know what you're saying. I just don't want anything to be wrong, and what if—"

"Stop it, Em. If there's something wrong with the baby, we'll deal with it."

She moved, but instead of pulling away, she rested her chin on his chest, looking up at him. "I never meant to insinuate that I blame you in any way, though I know I did."

He didn't know what to say, because he'd wondered. It had hurt to think either of them would stoop to blaming the other for something that was out of their control.

She licked her lips. "I want this baby, your baby." She shut her eyes for a second. "But I don't want to know if something is wrong. I don't want the amnio the doctor is pushing for."

He wondered for a moment, by the way she watched him, whether she was waiting for him to say something else or disagree with her. He couldn't do that. "Then no amnio it is."

She let out a sigh laced heavy with relief.

"Whatever is wrong or isn't, we'll deal with it when it comes," he said. "We'll take it one day at a time, and we won't worry this to death." He put his hands on her cheeks and just held her as she gazed up at him with such deep emotion that he could feel her heart reaching into his, touching it and settling in with him the way it always had been between them.

"Okay," she said. "I like that, I can work with that. Do you think—"

He pressed his hand to her mouth before she could voice the doubts he knew would plague her until the baby was born. "Don't say it. We don't know anything except that we're having a baby, and we'll love this baby and deal with whatever shows up. You know we can do it. It's just one more challenge."

This time she smiled. "Nothing could be wrong, too."

"Yeah, nothing could be wrong…but if something is, it's okay."

Chapter 26

Walking the ridge again, Brad had to make a decision about their family. An heir would need to take over, but there might never be someone suitable. Trevor could need a guardian, or the land might end up going to Neil, but for the first time Brad realized it didn't matter.

Emily was six months along, doing well, and they had settled in with their decision. Although the doctor had tried to change their mind, Brad had made it clear that if something was wrong with the baby, they would deal with it. He'd pointed out that this was their child and that sometimes knowing about a problem that hadn't yet happened could be worse. Emily had been watched closely since that day, with regular prenatal checkups, and both she and the baby had been doing well. In the end, that had been all Emily needed to hear.

As far as Katy, she was now dating Steven—with ground rules. The boy had shown up on his doorstep, where Brad had pulled him aside, speaking no nonsense and to the point, to tell him that if he had any ideas about talking Katy into letting him take her for a test drive, he'd better think again. Katy, at sixteen, was going to stay innocent for a while longer, and if Steven crossed that line, Brad would hunt him down and turn his life into a living hell. He'd seen the fear the boy took on the moment he understood Brad's meaning, but that hadn't kept him from stealing kisses with Katy every chance he got on the front porch as Brad and Emily sat in the living room, which was all the privacy they were willing to give them.

Tonight was a family dinner. Neil, Candy, and the kids were coming, and so was Steven. Brad was proud of himself for bending, but he figured the best way to keep Steven in line was to keep him close.

His phone rang in his jacket pocket, and he saw the home number.

"Where are you?" Emily teased.

"At the back of the property. I can see the house from where I am. I'm waving down to you now," he said.

"But I need you," she said, "and the kids won't be home for an hour. Everything is ready to be cooked for dinner."

He smiled as he lifted his rifle over his shoulder and started down the hill, knowing her need for him was from her raging hormones, as she'd said, making her want to have sex all the time. For Brad, that had been no hardship.

"On my way," he said as he hurried down the hill, making his way back home to his wife.

Chapter 27
LOOK WHO'S COMING FOR DINNER!

"**D**ad, Steven's here," Becky said. She was standing in the doorway, his precocious little girl with all the attitude of a young lady entering her teen years.

Brad pulled on a pair of socks where he sat at the edge of the bed, which was still a mess from having spent half an hour satisfying his wife before the kids came home—listening to her scream his name over and over as she leaned across the bed while he took her from behind. The kids…he wondered whether they knew, considering the number of showers he and Emily were taking during the day.

"He's coming for dinner. You knew that already," Brad said. "Is there something else?" He took in the look on her face, which was far from happy, and wondered for a moment whether she and Katy were fighting again. He stood up, pulling his boots on, taking in his damp hair from the shower he'd shared with Emily before she raced out after hearing the door and the kids on the stairs.

"He was kissing her again, and they were holding hands, and Katy got mad at me and told me to go away. That wasn't nice, Dad. And then they said I was spying on them, but I wasn't, I swear!" She sounded so hard done by when she took that attitude. He gave her a look like she should know better, and she just crossed her arms as if expecting him to do something.

Where were his boots? He had to look around and spotted them by the closet. He pulled them on. "Becky, give your sister some space. Cat will be here soon, and then you'll have someone to play with."

"But, Dad…" She started with the same dramatics he'd often seen in Katy, and he sighed.

Having girls was trying. He didn't understand their need to create a problem out of nothing, and Katy and Becky tested his patience at times. "Becky, I don't want to hear it anymore. Go downstairs. Give your mom a hand," he said, sliding his hand on Becky's shoulder and taking in her skinny jeans, long legs, and purple top. The problem was that it looked as if she was growing out of her clothes. Maybe this was something he should take off Emily's shoulders.

"Looks like your clothes are getting too small," he said as they started into the living room, which was empty. He could hear clatter and voices from the kitchen.

"I only have one pair of pants left I can get into. I told Mom. She said she'd get to it," Becky announced, again sounding as if it was the end of the world.

"Okay, maybe give your mom a break. I'll take you shopping in town, get you some clothes that fit."

"Take who shopping?" Emily looked up from where she was stirring something that smelled mighty good in a pot on the stove.

"Our daughter here." He took in Becky's face. She resembled Emily more and more every day but had Brad's dark hair, far different from her sister, Katy, who was all blond and slender. He looked up to see only Trevor in the kitchen with Emily, standing at the cutting board, slicing up a cucumber.

"Why do you need to take her shopping?" Emily was standing there, staring up at him in a black and white sleeveless silky top that draped nicely over her six-month rounded belly. Her face glowed, but he was sure that was from the sex they'd had not long ago. He swore she was more responsive now, being pregnant, than she'd ever been.

"Her clothes are too small. She's growing out of everything," Brad said, glancing to the back door. "Where're Katy and Steven?" He heard a vehicle pull in. *Must be Neil.*

"Katy…I think her and Steven went for a walk." Emily gestured to the back door. "Becky, I told you I would take you for new clothes as soon as you go through your drawers and pull out everything that doesn't fit you anymore. You have all your drawers shoved so full of clothes, nothing more will fit."

Brad heard footsteps, and the front door squeaked.

"Hello!" Neil called out.

Brad stepped back as Michael came running. He was getting big for three, and Cat was so tiny still, looking as if she could be in kindergarten when she was really nine. Both kids were dressed so neat and tidy. "Hey, guys, good to see you. Becky, take Michael with you and Cat."

He couldn't believe Becky rolled her eyes at him. "Dad, I want to play that new game with Cat, and Michael takes all our pieces and drives cars over the board."

"Go," he said as Neil bent down to say something to

Cat, signing. Candy slipped off her summer sweater, which was more for fashion than keeping her warm. She was wearing blue jeans, her long dark hair pulled up in a ponytail.

"You look nice," Brad said, noticing Cat and Becky on the stairs, giggling. Michael followed them.

"You told those two it was okay to go off together alone?" Brad said to Emily.

"Who are we talking about?" Neil asked.

"Steven and Katy," Emily said before giving Brad a look as if there wasn't a problem. She shrugged. "Why? They just wanted some time alone. They're fine, stop worrying." She glanced over to Trevor. "Oh, not that small, Trevor."

"Can I help with something?" Candy asked as she stepped into the kitchen.

Brad tapped Neil's shoulder. "Hey, Neil, take a walk with me."

"Sure," Neil said.

"Em, we'll be back," Brad said as he started to the back door, hearing the women in the kitchen, chatting, their attention elsewhere.

"So what's up?" Neil asked as they stepped outside. It was still warm out, but then, it was early August, and the warm days hadn't yet given way to cooler nights. It was comfortable, and he was glad for the cooler climate, being this close to the ocean and away from the scorching heat.

"Katy and Steven snuck off, I'm pretty sure, for a 'walk.' Just want to see where they went off," he said, shoving his hands in his pockets, feeling pulled in two different directions, one wanting to be with Emily, who was pregnant, and the other wanting to make sure Katy didn't end up the same. Steven was dropping by more and more as of late.

"Ah, so we're spying on the kids."

"No, more like keeping them on a short leash," Brad said.

"You have a talk yet with Steven?" Neil was walking beside Brad, dressed in dark jeans and a short-sleeved blue shirt. He was still tanned from going back and forth to Cancun. Brad had to take another look when he realized Neil had finally gotten a haircut, back to the neat and tidy and short style he always wore—along with the studded earring, a look that he didn't appear to want to let go of.

"What?" Neil asked.

"Still can't believe you got an earring and insist on wearing it all the time," Brad said. He had been sure it would be a passing phase. Boy, had he been wrong.

"Told you long ago, this is the new me. I've changed, like all of us," he said, shoving his hands in his pockets as they walked. He sighed, looking off in the distance. "So where do you suppose those two snuck off to?"

Brad took another look at Neil. Maybe there was something different about his brother. He just couldn't figure out what it was. "You okay?"

Neil didn't say anything for the longest time. Then he shrugged. "Yeah, I'm good." He said it a little too sharply for Brad's liking.

"You sure? Can always tell when something's off with you. You and Candy okay?"

This time Neil smiled, and he couldn't hide the sparkle in his eyes from Brad. The man loved his wife. So what was it?

"We're great—more than great, actually." He sighed again and then narrowed his eyes, looking off to the side as if he was holding on to something that was really bothering him.

"Is it the resort? Something going on I should know?"

Neil narrowed his eyes again and touched his tongue to his lip. Brad couldn't remember Neil being this bothered by something, not in this way. He wondered for a moment whether he'd glimpsed a sheen of tears in his brother's eyes. Now he was worried. Neil seemed to be fighting whatever this wave of emotion was. He stopped walking and faced Brad. They were away from the house and the other outbuildings.

"It's Candy," he said, then stopped as if he didn't want to say any more.

"What about her? Come on, spill it. Is something wrong? You're starting to worry me."

"We have two wonderful children I wouldn't trade for anything. I love them so much, and we had them in a way I'd never planned." He took a breath before giving all his attention to Brad again. Brad could see such sadness there, and for the life of him he didn't know why.

"With Emily being pregnant, it's hitting Candy kind of hard." Neil fisted his hands as if he was having trouble saying what he needed to, and Brad wasn't sure, for a moment, whether he wanted to hear it.

"Candy's been holding on to something for a while. I knew something was bothering her. I didn't push, because with Candy I need to give her time and space until she'll come to me. I'm just so glad we're in a place where she can now, where she will. With Emily being so messed up in the beginning when she found out she was pregnant, we gave her space, and we tried to be there for her. I thought it was just the way Emily was behaving at first, you know, all her craziness."

Brad was still struggling some days with what Emily had done, lashing out, behaving like an irrational teenager. He'd never expected it from her. It was the first time that she'd hurt him. "She turned us all upside down."

Neil crossed his arms. "I know she did. I know you two have a lot on your plate with the baby, what still could happen."

Brad didn't want to go there, not yet, anyways. Even though he'd told Emily they'd deal with whatever happened with the baby when it came, he wondered now whether that had been wise. He also knew she wasn't ready to deal with it. Emily needed to believe everything would be okay. Sometimes that worked, but there were times it wasn't practical.

"I found Candy on the bathroom floor last night, curled up in the corner, crying. She was trying to hide. I was putting the kids to bed, and…" Neil had to clear his throat, and his eyes teared up again as he took a sharp breath, doing his best to keep it together. "She's so torn up that she can't have children. I never realized how much she was hurting still. She wants a baby, she can't have one, and all I could do was just hold her and let her cry it out. She blames herself, thinks I still blame her for what happened, losing the baby, the hysterectomy. How could she think that?" He had to look away again, working the lump in his throat.

"Neil, I had no idea. You don't blame her, right? Because I know there was a time you did."

"You're right. I was a selfish bastard. I didn't deserve her, maybe still don't. It is what it is. We can't go back and change it. I wish I could, at times. I was so angry at her for so long, and I did blame her, even though I love her so much. Everything I did, I think I did it to hurt her, not consciously, but you know, the other level? I was so angry at her even though I kept telling myself I loved her, that it happened and I was over it, that we had to move on. The problem was that I never really admitted to myself every cruel thing I did, my possessiveness, jealousy, wanting to control her, shoving Maria in her face." He choked on the last part and uncrossed his arms, trying to get control of his emotions.

Brad had no idea how deep his brother's pain was, that it still lingered. "I don't know what to say, Neil. Why didn't you say anything?"

Neil's expression softened. "How could I say anything? I couldn't even admit to myself that everything I did, all the lies, the deceit, the blame, almost destroying us…it was because I still blamed her, but the reality was that in my fucked-up head, it was myself I blamed. I just never realized it until last night, when I was holding my wife as she sobbed and begged me to forgive her again. It was my fault, all of it. Never hers." This time Neil swiped at his eyes, then glanced out into the distance. "We should find Katy and Steven."

Brad's heart ached, and he knew Neil needed to change the subject. His brother wasn't one to show this kind of emotion. None of them were. It made them feel weak. He reached over and squeezed Neil's shoulder, feeling the tension and how tightly he was holding himself together. He wanted to say something, some words of wisdom, but what could he say that would make him feel better? "Let me know if there's anything I can do," he said.

This time, when Neil looked his way, Brad sensed a distance and something else he couldn't put his finger on. "You know what, Brad? Thanks, but I got this. Maybe this is what had to happen, but I know Candy and I are stronger than this, she's stronger. For the first time, I had to wonder whether I've screwed things up so badly because of me, my stuff, my issues, my guilt. I know now that we finally are at a place where we can put one foot in front of the other and move forward together."

A scream echoed.

The hair on the back of Brad's neck stood up. It was Katy, and all he could think was that Steven was with his daughter—and he was going to kill him.

Chapter 28

"Katy!" Brad shouted.

"It was coming from the barn," Neil said, running after him.

He heard whispers and shushing. "Katy, answer me right now!" he yelled. He couldn't remember feeling this kind of fear, which made him want to tear anything and everything apart in that moment.

Neil touched his shoulder. "Up there."

"Dad?" Katy was looking down from the loft, the big cutout in the floor. Darkness surrounded her, but he could see her hair was messed up.

"What's going on? Are you hurt? Why'd you scream?" He knew he sounded mad, but she'd scared him, maybe knocked another ten years off him, yet she looked fine. Her eyes were wide, staring down.

He gestured at the ladder. "Get on down here," he said, waving as she swung her foot onto it and stepped down, climbing down. Another foot behind her came Steven.

Brad glanced to Neil, who widened his eyes as the kids came down. So they'd snuck off alone together into the loft. Brad had a pretty good idea of what was going on. Katy stepped off the ladder, and he didn't miss how her shirt buttons were mismatched. She'd obviously done them up in a hurry. He had to look to Neil and could tell the moment he, too, noticed.

Steven jumped off the ladder—tall, lanky, the natural wave in his dark hair making it seem curly. He stood behind Katy. "Sorry about that," he said. "Katy saw a rat."

He had to give it to the kid for speaking up, not making Katy handle the situation. Well, sort of, considering he wanted to hurt the kid and ask questions later.

Katy swallowed, wide eyed, staring up at Brad. "I got scared. It jumped out at us. Didn't mean to scream like that," she said.

Brad raised an eyebrow and glanced down at her shirt buttons. Maybe she realized he'd figured out what they had really been doing in the loft, as she flushed. "Ah, Dad, we were just…"

"Yeah, don't even think about lying to me, Katy. Do you remember the rules we talked about for dating? And you!" He jabbed his finger at Steven. "I told you what would happen if you crossed a line with my daughter. She's barely sixteen, and you two snuck off so you could put your hands on her?"

Steven didn't step back or even try to hide. He did, though, appear terrified even when he stepped in front of Katy. Either he was stupid or there was something in him worth salvaging. "Sir, it didn't go that far. We were just…"

"Don't," Brad said just as Neil cleared his throat loudly.

The kid didn't move, but Katy put her hand on his

arm. "Dad, Steven is right. We just wanted to be alone without Becky dogging my heels and getting in our faces."

Brad held his hand out to Katy until she stepped around Steven. "Go in the house," he said, wondering for a moment whether she'd say no.

To her credit, she stepped closer and appeared worried. "Please, Dad…"

"Katy, go in the house. Steven and I need to have a word with each other. I've asked you once, I'm not asking again. Go." He gestured back through the barn door, realizing he hadn't lost all control of the situation.

Katy glanced pleadingly at Neil as she walked past, stopping once in the open barn doorway before running to the house.

When Brad glanced back at Steven, he was standing tall with his head up, shoulders back, and a fear in his eyes that made Brad feel pleased in an odd sort of way.

"You were having some fun up there with my niece, pushing the boundaries a little," Neil said.

Brad watched as the teen stood stoically. He didn't shuffle his feet side to side or look for an escape route, which he would have expected, since he was about five seconds shy of grabbing Steven and helping him find his way out of there.

"It didn't go that far. It could have, but we were just messing around, talking some. I love her," he said.

Brad wondered whether he was growling. Maybe Neil heard it, as he rested his hand on Brad's shoulder as if he needed to hold him back. "What the hell do you know about love, son? You're a kid."

"I'm seventeen, will be eighteen soon, and I plan to marry Katy one day," he said.

Of course Neil coughed, trying to cover up his laughter. Brad was still stuck on "love" and "marry" and the starry-eyed kid in front of him, who was obviously willing to stand in front of Brad and get his ass kicked. It said something about his character, bumping him up a notch in Brad's eyes from dung beetle to something more.

"I'd still like to stay for dinner, if that's all right with you, sir?"

Sir! He couldn't get over the kid's respect. He just stared at Steven, trying to figure out whether he was trying to play him or was merely idealistic. It was an admirable quality that would die eventually after life's hardships bit him in the ass a few hundred times.

"Yeah, go on, but no more sneaking off with my daughter, Steven, because if there's a next time, I'm not going to be so nice about it. Understand?" he said, taking a step closer. He was actually breathing down on the boy, who was a few inches shorter than he was.

Again, he didn't move, but Brad could tell it was taking everything in him not to jump back. That was another quality he liked: The boy never flinched. He met Brad's gaze so he could see the blue of his eyes, which were almost purple, his determination, and something else he wasn't sure he liked, because it reminded Brad of himself.

"Understood, sir," he said. Then he walked away but stopped in the doorway of the barn, looking back at Brad and Neil. "Thank you, Mr. Friessen." He turned around and walked back to the house.

Brad nearly sagged, feeling as if he'd gone a round or two in the ring. "This is going to be the death of me," he said, resting his arm against the ladder of the loft, staring over at his brother, who was doing his best not to laugh at him.

"I feel for you, brother, but you've got to give the kid credit."

"Why the hell should I?" he snapped.

Of course, Neil smiled wider. "Because he stood up to you, and that, my dear brother, is a sign that he just might be worth something."

Brad wanted to argue with Neil, but deep down, he knew he was right.

Chapter 29

Emily didn't know what was up with Brad, but she'd have been a fool not to notice the way he'd had his eye on Steven at dinner and, before Candy and Neil left, how he'd hugged her. It was only then that she'd realized something was going on. What had she missed now? Being so wrapped up in herself, the worries that something could go wrong with the baby or that she'd say or do something that would drive a wedge between her and Brad, was making her so self-absorbed that she was missing everything around her.

She drained the bath and reached for a plush navy bath towel, then dried herself, taking in her swollen belly in the mirror, how rounded it was. She rested her hand over it, feeling the familiar flutter. It squeezed at her heart, and her breath caught as the door opened and Brad walked in.

"Everything okay?" he asked, closing the door and then running his hand over her arm before moving behind her and sliding his arms around her, his hands over her hip, her belly, then her own hands.

She looked at him, the worry in his gaze reflecting back to her as she felt his strength around her. "Just feeling the baby kick," she said, needing to blank out all the overthinking she'd been doing—about the baby, about what she'd screw up next.

He was still watching her. Maybe he was waiting for her to go off again, but she'd been mindful not to do that, remembering all the hurt she'd put her husband through, and her family. She never wanted him doubting her again. She leaned into him as he ran his hand over her belly, holding her naked against him. She allowed the towel to fall to the floor, reaching up and touching his arm, holding on to him as if he was all that held her up.

"Anything else?" he asked, watching her closely.

She had to look down, and for a second she wanted to push away, walk away, but she knew he wouldn't let her. "If I say I'm not worried, you know it'll be a lie." She couldn't hide the sadness in her eyes. She sighed, reminding herself that it was the unknown that scared her. "But today everything is good," she said, forcing a smile, though she couldn't make it reach her eyes.

"What do you need right now to not worry?" He kissed her shoulder and then stepped back, pulling off his light T-shirt and dumping it in the hamper before he reached in and turned on the shower.

That was the million-dollar question. If this were a perfect world, she'd know everything was going to work out, but that wasn't reality. She shrugged. "I didn't want the amnio, all those tests, and I still wouldn't go back and make the choice to have it. It's just that not knowing what's around the corner scares the hell out of me lately. I'm trying not to think too hard."

He stepped closer, sliding his hand over her cheek so

she could lean in and hold on to his wrist. He didn't say anything, as he was so close, and he leaned down and touched his lips to hers. He pulled back. She couldn't keep from licking her lips, tasting him. He stepped away and pulled open the door to the shower.

"But I think you are holding on to something," she said. "Did something happen with Steven, the way you were watching him at dinner? Then there's Candy. I feel like I'm so wrapped up in myself, and you're not sharing when something happens or…" She stopped talking, because he still wasn't answering.

Brad stepped into the shower and dunked his head under the spray. He was washing his hair, and she wondered whether he was going to ignore her. "He surprised me," he said as he rinsed his hair, reaching for the soap.

"In what way?" She wondered what it was about Steven that had left her husband unsettled. She rather liked the boy who had Katy so googly eyed. As far as boyfriends for her daughter went, he wasn't all that bad. She leaned down, picked up the damp towel she'd dropped, and hung it on the rack before taking a second dry towel and holding it.

Brad turned off the shower, stepped out, and reached for the towel Emily was holding for him. He dried himself off.

"Brad, come on. I don't know what's going on," she said. This was starting to make her feel like the odd man out. She didn't like the fact that he kept things from her, even though he'd said that at times there were some things he'd just handle.

"I found them in the barn, up in the loft, fooling around, and the kid had the nerve to stand up to me when

I called them out. Wouldn't let Katy take the heat. Don't know if the kid is stupid…" Brad was now shaking his head. He let out a rough laugh before running the towel over his short hair and hanging it up. He started toward her, taking her hand and pulling her closer. "Said he plans on marrying her."

"What?" She went to pull away, press her hand to Brad's chest, but he just held her closer. Her daughter was just a kid. This was not happening.

"Hey, calm down. I don't want you getting all worked up. Besides, they're young. Lots of things could change," Brad said. "But I've got to admire the kid's determination. He was terrified, standing there with Neil and me breathing down his neck, but he didn't flinch. He stood there as if he'd made peace and would deal with getting his ass kicked. It's admirable, that trait—stupid, maybe." He was smiling again in a way that made Emily nervous.

"She's going to college, Brad, after high school. Marriage is a long ways off," Emily said.

He leaned against the counter, pulling her closer to him until she stood between his legs. "I guess that's another thing we've never talked about. Katy has never told us what she wants to do. Maybe it's time we ask her."

"What does she know of what she wants? She's only—"

"Hey, stop it." Brad rested his hands on her arms, holding her. "Katy may be so starry eyed over Steven that you telling her what she has to do instead of understanding what she wants to do will only backfire. We need to help her reach her goals, achieve her dreams. Don't push too hard, Em, based on what you want for her, that her dreams get buried."

"But I know better. She doesn't understand she has choices, and I want her to be able to have something for her, something to fall back on. I never went to college or university or had something of my own. I want her to have better." She wanted to bite her tongue as soon as she'd said the words, because they'd come out all wrong. She knew Brad had taken it in a way she hadn't intended by the odd look on his face. She wondered whether she'd just screwed things up again.

"So are you not happy now? Is that what you're saying?"

No, she was happy. Why was she making such a mess of this? He went to step away, and she squeezed her hands around his arm, holding on. "No, I didn't mean it that way. I'm screwing this up again, aren't I?"

He lifted his hand and skimmed her cheek. "What is it, then, you're trying to say?"

"Being married to you, being your wife, is my dream. Having a family, it's what I want. It's just that before you…" She didn't want to bring Bob into the equation or have her ex here with her and Brad right now. "I just don't want Katy making my mistake. You're my everything."

Maybe he finally understood what she was saying, as he was holding her. A smile lit up his face as he leaned down, his lips touching hers. He pulled her closer, and she had to reach up and loop her hands around his neck, leaning up, feeling all his hardness.

"I guess I'm just being silly, aren't I? She's only sixteen, and everything we're talking about is a long ways off." She ran her hand over Brad's chest, rubbing in circles. She needed to touch him, have his hands on her, because he made her feel so alive. "But I'm not, and I'm feeling a little needy right now." Her voice was husky as she felt his hands on her hips, sliding her around, holding her so close she knew he would have her in bed in a manner of moments, feeling his love and having her scream out his name.

Brad reached for the door and pulled it open. "Well, then, I'd say I'd better take you to bed and do something about that, Mrs. Friessen." He ran his hand over her bottom as she leaned up and touched her lips to his again, and he pulled her out of the bathroom, holding her hand, and took her to bed.

Chapter 30

It was her hand that woke him, stirring him from a dream as she ran it up the inside of his thigh. He didn't need to open his eyes to know her touch, but he did finally, sucking in a breath as he stretched. It was still dark. The sun hadn't quite reached the rise on the horizon. When she took hold of him, he wanted to roll his eyes back in his head. It wasn't a slow tease this morning as she kissed his chest and then climbed on, sliding all her sweetness down around him. His hands went to her hips, holding her as a gasp and a soft sigh escaped. He didn't need the light to see the need on his wife's face.

He reached up and touched her face, brushing her hair back. As she rose and settled again, she pressed a kiss to his palm, and he knew he'd never tire of waking this way. She was spoiling him even though he knew she was taking him for her own need.

When she cried out and went to collapse on top of him, he was far from done, so he rolled her over, still buried inside her. The baby bump between them had him leaning over her, holding her knees back, her head pressed back into the pillow, her hands by her head, her expression pure ecstasy. He moved inside her, taking her again and bringing her with him on this wild ride, feeling nothing and everything in that moment, just the two of them bringing in the morning the best way he knew how.

He didn't know how long he lay there in the silence, listening to her breathing, snuggled against him, her leg tossed over his, her hand on his chest, every part of her touching him as he held her close to him. He couldn't help reaching down and touching the baby growing between them, wondering about a lot of things whether it was a girl or a boy, what it would be like, and what they'd have to face. He couldn't imagine tossing a child away, not now, now that they'd bonded together. How could he? This baby was real now. The baby was his child, Emily's, theirs together. This child would be loved.

"I should get up," he said, knowing she was awake, that she was lying there, too, thinking.

"Or you could stay here a while yet. Is something going on with Neil and Candy? You never answered me last night. We talked about Steven and then you got me side-tracked."

It was more that she'd gotten him sidetracked by the number of times she'd come apart around him. She was explosive, needy, responsive, and their sex life now had gone from being already fantastic to mind blowing. He wondered how long he'd be able to keep up this pace. He held her tighter and pressed a kiss to her forehead, wondering what to share with her from what Neil had said. It was so raw, and he'd ached inside with worry about how Emily's pregnancy had opened a wound between Candy and Neil. How could he tell her?

She rustled beside him, sitting up, touching him and pushing back her hair. "What is it? You're starting to worry me. I know when you're holding something back. Please don't. We promised we'd share, so please don't start hiding things from me. Is there something wrong? Because now I'm really starting to panic."

He wanted to get up, move away. It was hard lying there and seeing how her expression was filled with such hurt. He knew with how erratic her hormones were, she would be all over the place in a few seconds, overthinking things.

"It's just something Neil shared with me. It was personal. Candy has a lot of unresolved issues. So does Neil, and…" She had come to a breaking point because Emily was pregnant with his child and she could never carry one. He couldn't imagine that kind of heartache.

"What unresolved issues? Please don't leave me out, because it's a lonely place and makes me feel as if you don't trust me."

Of course she'd take it this way, but how much worse would it be if she knew how Candy struggled to hold it together, hiding her feelings from everyone? "I do trust you. I just don't want you to take this the wrong way."

"Why would I take it the wrong way when I don't even know what it is I'm supposed to know? Now I'm starting to worry. You have to tell me, or maybe I should call Candy, go see her."

He reached for her arms, holding her. "No, don't do that. It's you being pregnant. When she saw it, all her hurt and Neil's, too, about the fact that they can't have children kind of came out. They thought they had resolved all that. Neil thought Candy was okay, but I guess he never really understood how much she was still hurting—or how much he was, too." He could feel her pull back. He didn't want that happening, of course not. "It's not your fault, so don't take it on," he added, knowing she would take it personally, wishing he'd kept it to himself. "I shouldn't have said anything."

"Of course you should have. I don't know how to feel about this. What should I do? I should talk to Candy." Emily fisted her hand on his chest, and he ran his hand over it, touching her, feeling all her worry, all her hurt, trying to get her to relax.

"No, you shouldn't. It's not really about you or me," he said. He didn't miss her expression even in the dimness of the room, how she wanted to argue with him about how wrong he was. "You were just the trigger for her," he said. The idea of Neil finding Candy the way he had…Brad ached that she was suffering so, but maybe this was what they needed to continue growing stronger together.

"I never wanted to really imagine what Candy was going through, what she was experiencing, because I was afraid of something like that happening to me," Emily said. "I wouldn't know how to handle it. I wouldn't know what to do. But I always thought she was so strong, how she'd gotten through it, held herself together through all the troubles she and Neil had."

Brad just lay there in the silence. He could tell Emily was thinking. He always knew when her mind was working on something. She flattened her hand on his chest.

"But you're wrong," she said. "I'm going to call Candy, talk to her." She scooted back and over to the side of the bed, away from him, before he could reach her again.

"No, Emily, don't call her and bring this up. It's a private moment. Candy didn't share it with me."

"But Neil did," Emily said, pulling on her bathrobe.

"Yeah, my brother shared his hurt, and I don't want him ever feeling as if I betrayed his confidence, so don't bring it up," he said again, realizing he needed Emily not to go off on something at a time when she wasn't thinking clearly about what was coming out of her mouth.

"Seriously, Brad? I'm not going to go over to Candy and tell her what you said. I know better."

Now he was confused. He didn't like this feeling of uncertainty about his wife, not knowing where her head was at and what she was going to say or do next. "Then what are you going to do?" He rolled over on his side and leaned up on his arm.

She glanced over at him after flicking on the bathroom light, which silhouetted her. "I'm going to call Candy and reach out to her and listen to what she doesn't tell me. That's what I'm going to do."

All Brad could do as Emily slipped into the bathroom was stare, lost, trying to figure out what the hell she meant by that. Maybe he should call Neil, at the very least warn him. Oh, yeah, that was definitely the wisest move, since he was the one responsible for sharing something that hadn't been his to share. Now he felt torn between his brother, Candy, and his wife. He had shared something private and personal at a time when Emily wasn't thinking as clearly as she should.

Chapter 31

He'd kept an eye on the house. In fact, he'd hidden Emily's keys to the van and the truck just so she couldn't slip off without him knowing. He hadn't had a chance to call Neil until an hour ago, and Neil's cell phone had gone to voicemail twice, so he'd left a little warning message and hoped Neil wouldn't be too angry.

He was crazy busy today, considering he had a ranch to run, cattle to move, and ranch hands to oversee. There had been a calf born, too, at an odd time of year. The horses had all had their hooves trimmed, and two of them had been reshoed with a visit from the farrier.

He started back to the house, mainly because he was hungry, surprised it was past lunchtime and Emily hadn't called once. She usually called him on his cell phone to remind him lunch was ready.

He pulled open the screen door, expecting some noise and chatter, considering the kids had another week of summer before heading back to school, but the kitchen was clean, the table clear, and Katy was bent over in the fridge before shutting the door. She was in a light tank top that showed her growing bust, barefoot in jean shorts that were a little too short for Brad's liking, and her very long blond hair was pulled back in a ponytail. She took a bite of an apple and glanced up, her blue eyes still filled with innocence. Why did he keep looking for that? He wondered whether he'd know when it changed. Yeah, he was sure he would, because right now there was nothing in her expression that showed any worry about the shelter he provided for his family, and he meant to keep it that way.

"Where is everyone?" He went to the sink and washed his hands.

"Aunt Candy came over and picked up Mom. They took Becky shopping for new clothes. Trevor went, too."

He turned off the water and stared over to Katy, wondering whether she could see the fact that he'd been outsmarted by his wife. He let out a chuckle.

"What?" Katy was wide eyed. Obviously, she had no idea.

He dug into his pocket and pulled out both sets of keys, putting them back on the hook. He was shaking his head. "Your mom call Candy?" he asked.

"Yeah." She stared at the keys, pointing. "Mom was looking for those."

He was sure she had been, and she'd obviously figured out he was trying to stop her from going.

"Dad, did you try to hide Mom's keys from her?"

"And if I did?" he asked her teasingly as he leaned back against the counter.

Katy took another bite of her apple, chewing as if thinking. "That wasn't very nice, but I get it." She shrugged.

Brad went to the fridge and pulled it open, then glanced over his shoulder to Katy. "How come you didn't go?" He spotted the leftover chili from two nights ago and pulled it out. He reached for a bowl in the cupboard, waiting for Katy to say something, before she shrugged as if knowing he could see.

"I didn't want to. Just wanted some space."

"Everything okay?" At times, with Katy, it was like pulling teeth, trying to get her to open up. How things had changed in a few short years. Before, she'd never stopped talking, sharing.

"Mom said she wants me to start thinking about college and what I want to do. She said I have to start pulling up my grades or I won't get into a good school." She was crossing her arms, and her expression was a little troubled.

Brad scooped chili into a bowl and tossed a paper towel overtop before sticking it in the microwave. "She did?" He had to bite his tongue, because he'd just spoken with Emily the night before about Katy, the future, and school. He'd wanted to sit Katy down for a talk about what she wanted. "So what do you want to do?"

Katy strode to the counter, put her apple down, and looked up at Brad. "Dad, I don't want to go to some fancy school and sit in a bunch of boring classes. Why do I have to decide now? I sure don't want to be some doctor or take a bunch of administrative courses to be some high-powered executive."

Where was she getting this? Maybe he frowned when he glanced down at her. The microwave dinged, and he pulled out the steaming bowl and set it on the counter, as it burned his fingers. He noticed how bothered she seemed. "Why would you have to be any of those? You be what you want to be, Katy, as long as it makes you happy. What do you want to do? You must have some idea? You're old enough now to know what you want to do and be. You must have some dream about something." He reached into the drawer for a spoon and set it in the steaming bowl.

"Well, Mom seemed pretty excited when she talked about me being a doctor or getting my MBA like Uncle Neil."

Brad was stirring the steaming chili and froze, looking ever so slowly over to Katy. Had Emily not heard a word he'd said? "Of course that would be nice, but only if that's what you want to do, Katy. I'm sure your mom didn't mean it like that. Anything you want to do would be fine, too. It's not about me and your mom and what we want you to do, it's about what you want to do. What makes you excited? Have you thought about it?" He was really going to have to sit Emily down. He understood she only wanted the best for Katy, but pushing her to something she believed would be good for her was so wrong on so many levels. He needed to get her to understand this wasn't about her. This was about Katy.

"I don't want to go to college, Dad. I know that." She looked away and picked up her apple, and the way she stood there, he knew she wasn't sharing everything.

"Katy, come on, what else? You don't want to go to college, okay," he said, but he knew it wasn't, really. He was having to hold back what he was really feeling—that without an education, her options would be limited, leaving her to pick up the sort of minimum-wage jobs that weren't on anyone's aspiration list. She needed to understand he wasn't going to drive her in a direction she didn't want to go, though, or she'd never figure out what she really wanted.

Maybe he surprised her, as her eyes widened and she licked her lips. "Steven and I were talking, and..." She hesitated at the same time Brad felt his back stiffening. He wasn't sure he was going to like this, but he didn't want her shutting down, either.

"You and Steven were talking about what, Katy?"

"You promise you won't get mad?"

How was he going to promise something like that when he was in the dark? "Katy, just tell me already. You should know, if anything, you can always talk to me. I'm always going to listen. Why do you think I'm going to get mad?"

She crossed her arms across her skinny chest. "Because Steven and I want the same things. We were talking about after we finish high school…" She hesitated again.

"Go on. After high school, you were talking about plans for…." He gestured between them. "I presume this is something about the two of you."

"We'd like to have a small place like you, Dad, a ranch. Steven's granddad is a farmer, always has been, and Steven wants to have his own ranch, do some farming, just like you. We want to be like you and Mom and get married when I'm eighteen."

Brad squeezed the spoon, reminding himself to breathe.

Before he could say anything, he heard the door—bags, kids, and Emily. He put his hand on Katy's shoulder. "Why don't we talk about this again tonight? Katy, I do want to talk about this, because there are a lot of steps to take to get to what you're talking about."

"So you're not mad?" She was looking up at him and then over to the doorway, where Emily appeared, carrying two bags, wearing a bright smile before she took in Brad and Katy.

"What's going on?" she asked.

For the first time ever, Brad realized that what Katy had shared wasn't something he could share with Emily right now. He glanced down at Katy, not missing the worry she had about Emily finding out what she'd said. "Just talk-ing," he said. "Where'd you sneak off to?"

She firmed her lips. "Shopping for your daughter, who grew out of all her clothes." She pulled out clothes from the bag and was saying something to Becky and Trevor as she walked around Brad to the fridge, distracted. Brad said nothing else as he took in Katy and the relief that passed in her eyes at the fact that he'd kept her dream, the thing she had confided in him, to himself.

Chapter 32

So Brad had thought he was outsmarting her by hiding the keys. She knew he'd hidden them when all the keys had suddenly disappeared from the key rack. It was so obvious, his move, not wanting her to talk to Candy. The man gave her no credit at all. The fact he thought she'd bring up Candy's heartache and sorrow, something Candy herself hadn't shared with Brad, something he had only heard through Neil, it was like he didn't understand her at all.

She'd spent a wonderful morning shopping, buying clothes for Becky. Candy had driven them, and it had just been the usual time spent with her sister-in-law, who Emily was closer with than two sisters could be. She loved Candy. She was her friend, her confidante at times, and she knew Candy held on to a lot of things until she was ready to talk. The entire morning they'd been out, Candy had never shared anything of her sorrow. In fact, if Brad hadn't told her, Emily wouldn't have believed Candy was harboring such heartache.

Emily had her feet up on the stool on the front deck, lounging in the soft cushioned chair. She put down the book she'd been reading, taking a listen to the sounds around her: a tractor in the distance, sounds from the cattle, everything one might hear on a ranch on a warm August day. She loved this life and wouldn't trade it for anything.

The sun was bright, and the kids were off somewhere on the ranch, helping Brad. She noticed Katy on the tractor, pulling in and parking by the barn. Brad came out and said something to her, and the other two kids were helping with bales of hay, stacking and loading. It made her smile.

She could hear a car pulling into the driveway and noticed the blue Cavalier, the older model that Steven drove. He climbed out, waved to Emily, and looked over to the barn.

"Hi, Steven," Emily called out before he could take off to where Katy was.

"Hi, Mrs. Friessen. I hope it's okay I just dropped by?"

"Of course," she said, putting her hand on the baby, feeling the kick.

Steven looked toward the barn and back to her, shoving his hands in his jeans pockets. His light blue T-shirt was a little baggy, but he was tall and good looking, wearing boots much like her husband wore. He started toward her, and she realized he had cut his dark hair, a short cut just like Brad's. She had to hide her smile.

"How are you feeling today?" Steven asked, gesturing to the baby she carried inside her.

"We're good today. Thanks, Steven. So what are you up to?"

"Just got off work. I'm working part time at the hardware store, but I was hoping I could give Katy's dad a hand here at the ranch. My mom and dad aren't much for the country life. My dad owns the seaside restaurant, but my grandad always farmed and had animals. I loved helping him." Steven smiled as he stood on the bottom step, his hand on the white post.

"Yeah, Katy mentioned your dad owned a restaurant. So what are your plans this year? You're going into twelfth grade, your senior year. What colleges or universities are you planning for?"

She'd never had one-on-one time with Steven to find out about his long-term goals, what his plans were for the future. She was feeling a need now after the little bomb Brad had dropped on her last night. Marriage, seriously? They were just kids!

"I'm thinking more a trade school. I love working with my hands, and then eventually I'd like to have something like you and Mr. Friessen have, my own place like this, working the land."

She didn't know why that made her uncomfortable, but Steven was a year older than Katy, and she was hoping he'd have higher aspirations. She didn't know why, but she pictured Katy having more, being with someone who had more.

"Katy and I have talked about it a lot, and what you and Mr. Friessen have here is something we want." He was smiling, and she wasn't sure what he was prattling on about now, because she was still stuck on the "we" part.

"Having a place like this would cost a small fortune, and then there's running it, but then, I suppose you could be a ranch hand to start with for the experience," Emily said. "I'm not sure I'm seeing how you and Katy expect to have something like this." She put her book down on the small table beside her and stuck her feet back in her sandals just as she heard Katy call out Steven's name. He waved and stepped down.

"I'm going to go see Katy, if that's all right." He was being polite, which she liked, but for the first time, she didn't like his lack of ambition. Why couldn't he have a burning desire to be a doctor, a lawyer, something other than trade school?

"I'll walk over with you." She started down the steps, walking with Steven, who was talking beside her about the weather tomorrow, or maybe it was something blowing in. She didn't have any idea of what it was, because she'd stopped listening to him. She dug in to each step closer to her husband, to Katy.

Brad was just coming out of the barn with a bale of hay and tossed it on the back of the trailer. "Hey, Steven! Why don't you grab the last two bales and load it up?" He tossed his gloves to Steven, who grabbed them and went into the barn with Katy.

Brad wiped the sweat from his forehead with the back of his arm. "Everything all right?" he asked, looking down at Emily. She swiped at a bee that buzzed her bare leg and pulled at the elastic of her maternity shorts, which pinched.

"Steven just told me something a little troubling." She stood in front of Brad and took in his frown as he glanced over his shoulder and then slid his hand on her arm.

"What is it?"

"He and Katy have been talking and want to have a place like this. He's maybe looking at trade school. For what, I don't know. It sounds as if he has my daughter convinced our life is the life for them. What kind of dream world is he living in? And Katy…he could be leading her down a path where she's going to turn away from being someone truly special." Emily could feel herself getting worked up, and Brad rested his hand on her shoulder and didn't seem at all surprised by what she was saying. "Did you know?" she asked, but of course he wouldn't say something. This was her daughter.

"Calm down," he said. "Katy mentioned something to me before you came home. We hadn't finished talking. They have a dream, Emily, and I never said it was smart, but who are you and I to say what's best for them? Anything could change between now and then," he added in a low voice. Maybe he didn't want anyone to hear, but Emily couldn't help being furious that he hadn't told her.

"You should have said something to me, Brad. Now who's keeping secrets? Katy is going to college. She's getting a degree so she can be somebody," Emily said.

Brad just stood there, shaking his head as if he was going to argue with her. "You can't decide for Katy what she's going to do, Em. You have to let her figure out her dreams, and pushing her to be like Neil, the Harvard graduate, or to be a doctor isn't fair. That's your wish, Emily— and seriously, Em, what's wrong with trade school?"

"There's nothing wrong with it. I just don't want that for my daughter. I want her with someone who's ambitious, who knows what he wants in life. I don't want Katy to ever be with someone who makes her feel as if she isn't good enough, someone who leaves her to figure everything out herself, to handle it all. I want her to have someone who's carved out his own way, someone educated, ambitious, and for her to have her own niche, too. I don't ever want her to end up with nobody like I did, suffering that kind of loneliness. Is that so much to ask?" She was out of breath and didn't realize she'd been yelling. Becky and Trevor were standing there with a bale of hay between them, and Katy was standing beside Steven, both with a look of hurt as if Emily had taken something precious away.

Everybody was watching her as if no one knew what to say, and in that moment she wished she could take back what she'd said, take the hurt off her daughter's face. "Katy, I'm sorry."

"Mom, I knew you never liked Dad, but he's still my dad—and so are you, Dad. You think I don't know how you feel? I'm not you, Mom, and I know my dad isn't the kind of man with ambition or someone who can look after a family, I get that, but I have a great dad now in Brad. I wouldn't trade him for anything. It's Dad and you who've shown me what real love is, so what is so wrong with me wanting what you have?" She was crying, and it hurt Emily to think she'd done that to her daughter.

"There's nothing wrong with that, Katy," Brad said as he held out his arm, and she went to him and hugged him. Steven was still there, watching, looking uncomfortable and humiliated, but he wasn't looking to leave.

"I just don't want you making any mistakes like I did," Emily said, and she didn't miss the look in Brad's eyes, his expression warning her to stop.

"Mom, I'm not you. I wouldn't make a mistake like you did."

For the first time, Emily felt as if her daughter had slapped her, and she backed up.

"Don't talk to your mother like that," Brad said gently, but Emily was already turning a little too fast, her sandal catching in a groove in the ground. She tripped, feeling herself falling. She hit the ground on her belly, her elbow skimming the gravel, her face in the dirt. She heard Brad yell, and one of the kids.

"Em, are you okay?" he asked, helping her sit up. For a minute, she was too stunned to say anything as she brushed at the dirt on her shorts, feeling shock more than anything else.

"I think I'm fine, just lost my footing and tripped."

"Mom, are you sure you're okay?" Katy had her hand on her shoulder, and then Becky was touching her arm.

"Just help me up. I'm fine." She looked over to Brad as he held her arms and helped her to her feet, and she didn't miss the worry in his expression. She was shaky as she stood there. "Just help me back to the house. I think I just want to lie down for a minute."

She was being lifted by Brad, and she put her arm around his neck, leaned her head on his shoulder.

"Steven, open the door for me," Brad said. "Katy, Trevor, Becky, let's get your mom inside." Everyone was there fussing as Brad put Emily on the sofa. "You landed really hard on the baby. I think we need to go in to the hospital."

"Mom, your arm is bleeding," Becky said. Katy lifted her arm, and Emily saw the scrape with a bit of blood.

"I just need a cloth and some antiseptic. It's fine, just a scrape. Katy, why don't you run up to the bathroom and grab that for me?"

Brad was dialing the phone.

"Who are you calling?" Emily asked.

Brad looked at Steven and gestured to the stairs. "Go grab a pillow from my room, bring it down." Brad had the phone pressed to his ear. "I'm calling your doctor."

Emily didn't know where to look as Becky scooted beside her. Trevor had his hand on her forehead.

"Nope, not hot," he said. "You okay, Mom?"

"I'm fine, Trevor," she said as Katy raced down the stairs, Steven behind her. Brad now had his back to her, talking to the doctor, while Steven put a pillow behind her. Katy dabbed at her arm, and Trevor hovered.

"Okay, we're going to the hospital," Brad said. "Doctor Keyes is meeting us there. Katy and Steven, you stay here and look after Becky and Trevor." Brad bent down to lift Emily in his arms just as she felt a cramp in her belly that sucked her breath away.

"Oh no!" she cried out.

Chapter 33

Brad couldn't remember ever being so terrified of anything in his life. Of all the heartache he'd lived through, he and Emily had climbed mountains to be together, raising a family that was far from typical—whatever that meant anymore. He wouldn't trade anything in their life.

Emily had been put on bed rest. The trauma of the fall had triggered early labor, which the doctor had stopped, but she'd been confined to bed for the remainder of her pregnancy, which had the entire family stepping up. Katy and Becky spent time after school just lying in bed with her, sharing their day. Trevor had convinced Emily that watching DC and Marvel movies was the sure thing to cure her. The kids watched TV with Emily, read to her, talked to her, and when Brad carried Emily down the stairs for dinner every day, not letting her walk except to go to the bathroom, the family gathered. Even Steven seemed to spend most nights at the dinner table with the family.

His mom and dad flew in. Neil and Candy stopped in almost every day, and he'd seen how Candy holed up with

Emily for hours some days. Whatever it was those two talked about, it had kept Emily sane and put her in a frame of mind that was more at peace. Of course, though, there were days her frustration gave way to tears.

After sixty-three days of bed rest, of being waited on by family and having everyone around her, Emily's water had broken. With the family in the waiting room, Brad held Emily's hand. Her hair was damp, and sweat beaded her forehead as she struggled through her painful contractions.

"Come on, Emily, push," Brad said again, sitting behind her.

"Okay, baby's almost out," the doctor said. "One more push, Emily."

She struggled and screamed out, and the doctor cut the cord and laid the baby on her belly.

"It's a boy!" he said. "Congratulations, Mom, Dad. Just give me a second here, and we're going to check him out."

"Oh, Brad, look at him," Emily said. The emotion in her voice got to him, and he had to clear his throat as the nurse wiped the blood from his son's face and then lifted him from Emily.

"I'll give him right back," she said.

"He looks good, right, doc?" Brad said, hoping the doctor would say something positive.

"Apgar is a nine," the doctor said. He had a big smile on his face. "Looks good." He nodded to Brad, and of course Emily started crying.

EMILY HAD BEEN CLEANED up and was still in the family birthing room when the door popped open. She was holding her baby after counting his fingers and toes and checking him over not once but twice. Afterward, the doctor had assured them everything looked good and whatever had showed up in the early days on the blood test had been a false positive, but he did insist that having an amnio would have ruled out the worry.

Brad had snapped right back, "And it was our choice not to have one."

She loved him for that.

"You up for visitors?" Brad said as he walked in, and her eyes misted when Katy, Becky, and Trevor filed in, Brad's parents with them, along with Neil and Candy. It was the entire family. They were just missing Diana and Jed, who had their three boys now, and Andy and Laura, who were off in Montana, but having everyone else here meant so much that Emily couldn't help the mist of tears that burned her eyes.

"Oh, look at him! He looks just like you did, Brad, when you were born," Brad's mom said. "How are you doing, Emily?" She rested her hand on Emily's leg as Katy came around the other side, looking down at the baby and back at Emily.

"You okay, Mom?" she asked. Emily had apologized to Katy for her thoughtless remarks several times, but her daughter hadn't allowed it to come between them. She loved her, she loved her entire family.

"I'm good," Emily said, "and so is your brother."

Candy came around the side of the bed behind Katy, looking down at the baby, a mist in her eyes. She looked back at Emily. "See? Just what I told you: Things have a way of working out, just not in the way we plan."

"Yeah," Emily said. She swallowed, because Candy had never shared with Emily her moment of sorrow. Emily realized there were some things everyone was entitled to keep to themselves.

"So what's his name?" Neil asked, resting his hands on his mom's shoulder. Rodney stood at the foot of the bed, watching Emily like the proud grandfather he was.

"Do you want to tell them?" Emily looked up to Brad, who was standing beside her, Trevor and Becky in front of him, just as a knock sounded at the door. Everyone looked over, but it was Neil who went to the door and whispered to someone. There was Steven, who walked around the bed to Katy, holding a camera. "Don't even think of taking my photo!" Emily said, though she admired his determination.

Apparently so did Brad, as he smiled over at him. "Glad you could come, Steven. Everyone, I want you to meet the newest Friessen. This is Jack."

Turn the page for a sneak peek of
FIRST LOVE the next book in *THE FRIESSENS*
Available in print, eBook and Audiobook.

"Best family series ever! I love the dynamic of this powerful close family. Three brothers, a cousin, and all the spouses and children make for an interesting, spellbinding story you won't want to put down."

Amazon Customer

"This is a series that you will go back to time and again to reread. Lorhainne Eckhart is that type of writer. Love her stories about family and their journey. This is a great read, full of love for family that sticks together."

Joann Moore

"I have read all of Lorhainne Eckhart's Outsiders and Friessens books. I rarely read the same book more than once, but have read the entire Outsiders series twice. Ms. Eckhart's books are so filled with raw emotion and family relationships and all of those dynamics."

Aherman

EVERYONE SAID THEY WERE TOO YOUNG TO LOVE.

Katy and Steven have planned out their happily ever after: marriage, family, and a place of their own. A simple life in a small town with big dreams, just like Katy's parents, Brad and Emily.

However, life's hardships soon threaten the future Steven and Katy have planned together.

Yellow was Katy's favorite color, and having the sun stream in the bedroom window, casting light over the white walls and the vivid yellow print of her duvet first thing in the morning, brought a smile to her face. She stretched and, like every morning, could hear voices outside on the ranch, clatter downstairs from her mom cooking, and then the familiar call of "Katy, Becky, time to get up!" Trevor, her older brother, who had autism, would already be up, of course, as he was every morning.

Her mom was Emily Friessen, formerly Nelson, and Katy still carried her other dad's name—not that Brad wasn't her dad. Technically, he was her stepdad, and he had become her legal guardian, taking care of the question of who was responsible for her if something happened to Emily. Her name now told the story: Katy Nelson-Friessen. Brad would always be the father who had raised her, had been there for her through all the good, the bad, and the everyday events of life. He was the father she needed, trusted, looked up to, the one she went to for everything.

Her real dad lived up in Olympia, and she saw him as

often as she could, but he just stayed in touch and played a background role in her life. He was not the type who, when push came to shove, would stand and fight for her or be the watchdog at her door. That was Brad. No, Katy's birth father, Bob Nelson, wasn't made that way. He loved her, but he had a life elsewhere and didn't have an alpha bone in his body. Maybe that should have bothered her more, but it didn't. He was just her dad.

Katy had a home, a family, parents she loved and looked up to, a baby brother just learning to walk, a sister who annoyed her at times, and a stepbrother who was a few years older. She and Trevor were close. He counted on her, and she looked out for him. Helping him was second nature. Tomorrow she would be eighteen, graduating grade twelve in two weeks, and she was in love with Steven Bennett.

She knew people didn't take their commitment seriously and maybe considered them too young to understand what love was, but what they needed to understand was that Steven was her first love, her true love, her only love. Her cell phone buzzed from where she'd tucked it under her pillow. She didn't need to look to know who was calling, but his handsome face with dimples flashed on the screen.

"Hi," she said. She always felt her insides turn to mush at the sound of Steven's voice.

"Have you told your parents yet?" His deep voice had her wanting to wrap her arms a little tighter around her stomach, dreamily wishing he was there and that she could touch him. She loved the feel of him, his touch, his kiss, just being with him. She ached when he was gone.

"No. I will today, I promise," she said, glancing at her door, hearing the footsteps and fearing time was almost up.

"I should be there with you."

"Katy, I called you already…" Emily opened the door, gesturing at her because she had the phone stuck to her ear again. "Hang it up already. You need to be ready for school. You're not even dressed."

"Steven, I've got to go."

"Love you," he said, and she couldn't smother the big grin that swept across her face.

"I love you, too."

Her mom stepped into the bedroom. Her baby brother, Jack, was resting on her hip in just a diaper and T-shirt. His thick dark hair, unusual for a baby, was sticking straight up. He had Brad's expression, her mom's eyes, and a strong personality. She'd heard her mom say many times that Jack was stubborn and difficult just like the Friessen men.

She dropped her phone on the bed as she got up, her pale green nightgown riding higher as she slipped from bed. "Mom, can I get dressed?" she said, wondering about the way Emily was watching her, her expression. Katy knew her mom was wondering whether she was keeping something from her. She'd seen it a hundred times before as if her mom was trying to yank her back to being the little girl who had shared everything.

"So what's going on?" Emily said. "Steven's calling again, and so early." Her mom was making a face, and then something in her expression, around her eyes, seemed concerned. "I know we've talked about this love thing, how you think you and Steven are—"

"Oh my God, Mom, would you stop? We are in love," she snapped, interrupting Emily before she could tell her one more time how to feel, how it was impossible for someone almost eighteen to understand grownup love, how it was just infatuation. It hurt the way her mother made her feel she didn't know her own mind.

Even Brad had stepped in a few times and warned Emily to stop.

"Watch your mouth, Katy." Emily stepped back, frowning again, looking to the window. "Just hurry and get dressed or you're going to miss the bus, and I don't have time to drive you today." She started out the door but stopped, her hand on the doorknob as she faced Katy again.

"You know, Mom, I could drive myself—should drive myself. I don't understand why you have to treat me like a child. The few times you've let me get behind the wheel, it's a wonder I know how to drive at all." She'd even asked her dad if she could have a car, but he'd said no, as he'd gotten rid of all the old vehicles parked around the house except for her mom's minivan and his brand-new truck, one her mom didn't drive very often.

"You can when you have a car of your own—which you need a job to pay for. Oh, and to get a good job you need to have an education, so get dressed, hurry up, and maybe focus more on school today and less on Steven."

She just had to say it again, and now Katy couldn't help worrying about what else her mom was going to ram down her throat about how she thought she should feel or act. She didn't talk this way to Becky or Trevor, and Katy was beginning to resent her mom's interference more and more.

Maybe it was her growing frown, as she could feel her radiant good mood heading right into the trash, that had her mom sighing and backing out. "Never mind. Just get dressed," Emily said, and she closed the door behind her.

Katy couldn't help reaching for the phone again and dialing before she heard a tap on the door. It opened again.

"Oh, yeah, and no more phone tucked under your pillow, Katy. Your room is for sleeping, not talking on your cell phone. I want to see it downstairs from now on, plugged in with ours, or no more phone. Understand?"

Katy dumped the phone on the bed again, and this time when the door closed she went over and pressed the lock in the center of the brass handle. She leaned against the door and listened to her mom in the hallway, now on to Becky, nagging her about something she was wearing. Good! Katy smiled as she reached for her phone to call Steven again as she searched her closet for something to wear.

About the Author

"Lorhainne Eckhart is one of my go to authors when I want a guaranteed good book. So many twists and turns, but also so much love and such a strong sense of family."

(Lora W., Reviewer)

New York Times & USA Today bestseller Lorhainne Eckhart writes Raw Relatable Real Romance is best known for her big family romances series, where "Morals and family are running themes. Danger, romance, and a drive to do what is right will see you glued to the page." As one fan calls her, she is the "Queen of the family saga." (aherman) writing "the ups and downs of what goes on within a family but also with some suspense, angst and of course a bit of romance thrown in for good measure." Follow Lorhainne on Bookbub to receive alerts on New Releases and Sales and join her mailing list at LorhainneEck-hart.com for her Monday Blog, books news, giveaways and FREE reads. With over 120 books, audiobooks, and multiple series published and available at all retailers now translated into six languages. She is a multiple recipient of the Readers' Favorite Award for Suspense and Romance, and lives in the Pacific Northwest on an island, is the mother of three, her oldest has autism and she is an advocate for never giving up on your dreams.

"Lorhainne Eckhart has this uncanny way of just hitting the spot every time with her books."

(Caroline L., Reviewer)

The O'Connells: *The O'Connells of Livingston, Montana are not your typical family. A riveting collection of stories surrounding the ups and downs of what goes on within a family but also with some suspense, angst and of course a bit of romance thrown in for good measure "I thought I loved the Friessens, but I absolutely adore the O'Connell's. Each and every book has totally different genres of stories but the one thing in common is how she is able to wrap it around the family which is the heart of each story." (C. Logue)*

The Friessens: *An emotional big family romance series, the Friessen family siblings find their relationships tested, lay their hearts on the* *line, and discover lasting love! "Lorhainne Eckhart is one of my go to authors when I want a guaranteed good book. So many twists and turns, but also so much love and such a strong sense of family." (Lora W., Reviewer)*

The Parker Sisters: *The Parker Sisters are a close-knit family, and like any other family they have their ups and downs. "Eckhart has crafted another intense family drama…The character development is outstanding, and the emotional investment is high…" (Aherman, Reviewer)*

The McCabe Brothers: *Join the five McCabe siblings on their journeys to the dark and dangerous side of love! An intense, exhilarating collection of romantic thrillers you won't want to miss. — "Eckhart has a new series that is definitely worth the read. The queen of the family saga started this series with a spin-off of her wildly successful Friessen series." From a Readers' Favorite award—winning author and "queen of the family saga" (Aherman)*

Lorhainne loves to hear from her readers! You can connect with me at:
www.LorhainneEckhart.com
lorhainneeckhart.le@gmail.com

Also by Lorhainne Eckhart

The Outsider Series
The Forgotten Child (Brad and Emily)
A Baby and a Wedding *(An Outsider Series Short)*
Fallen Hero (Andy, Jed, and Diana)
The Search *(An Outsider Series Short)*
The Awakening (Andy and Laura)
Secrets (Jed and Diana)
Runaway (Andy and Laura)
Overdue *(An Outsider Series Short)*
The Unexpected Storm (Neil and Candy)
The Wedding (Neil and Candy)

The Friessens: A New Beginning
The Deadline (Andy and Laura)
The Price to Love (Neil and Candy)
A Different Kind of Love (Brad and Emily)
A Vow of Love, A Friessen Family Christmas

The Friessens
The Reunion
The Bloodline (Andy & Laura)
The Promise (Diana & Jed)
The Business Plan (Neil & Candy)
The Decision (Brad & Emily)
First Love (Katy)
Family First
Leave the Light On
In the Moment
In the Family

In the Silence
In the Charm
Unexpected Consequences
It Was Always You
The First Time I Saw You
Welcome to My Arms
Welcome to Boston
I'll Always Love You
Ground Rules
A Reason to Breathe
You Are My Everything
Anything For You
The Homecoming
Stay Away From My Daughter
The Bad Boy
A Place of Our Own
The Visitor
All About Devon
Long Past Dawn
How to Heal a Heart
Keep Me in Your Heart

The O'Connells
The Neighbor
The Third Call
The Secret Husband
The Quiet Day
The Commitment
The Missing Father
The Hometown Hero
Justice
The Family Secret
The Fallen O'Connell
The Return of the O'Connells

And The She Was Gone
The Stalker
The O'Connell Family Christmas
The Girl Next Door
Broken Promises
The Gatekeeper

The McCabe Brothers
Don't Stop Me (Vic)
Don't Catch Me (Chase)
Don't Run From Me (Aaron)
Don't Hide From Me (Luc)
Don't Leave Me (Claudia)
Out of Time

A Billy Jo McCabe Mystery
Nothing As it Seems
Hiding in Plain Sight
The Cold Case
The Trap
Above the Law
The Stranger at the Door
The Children
The Last Stand

The Wilde Brothers
The One (Joe and Margaret)
The Honeymoon, A Wilde Brothers Short
Friendly Fire (Logan and Julia)
Not Quite Married, A Wilde Brothers Short
A Matter of Trust (Ben and Carrie)
The Reckoning, A Wilde Brothers Christmas
Traded (Jake)
Unforgiven (Samuel)

The Holiday Bride

Married in Montana
His Promise
Love's Promise
A Promise of Forever

The Parker Sisters
Thrill of the Chase
The Dating Game
Play Hard to Get
What We Can't Have
Go Your Own Way
A June Wedding

Kate & Walker
One Night
Edge of Night
Last Night

Walk the Right Road Series
The Choice
Lost and Found
Merkaba
Bounty
Blown Away: The Final Chapter

The Saved Series
Saved
Vanished
Captured

Single Titles
He Came Back

Loving Christine

For my German Readers
Die Außenseiter-Reihe
Der Vergessene Junge
Der Gefallene Held

For my French Readers
L'ENFANT OUBLIÉ